Dear Diary,

Tonight I'm sneaking out of the house to be with Ben. Grounded or not, I need to see him. We're meeting on the beach. Diary, I'll fill you in on all the details when I get home . . .

The rest of the page was blank. "Oh, Rita! Be careful!" I whispered. "Don't let him hurt you!"

It was like reading a book where someone has told you the outcome. Yet, as I read Rita's words they sounded so immediate. It was almost as if she were there with me—talking to me.

She was going to be killed. And there was nothing I could do to stop it . . .

WHISPERS
FROM THE
GRAVE

Leslie Rule

BERKLEY BOOKS, NEW YORK

WHISPERS FROM THE GRAVE

A Berkley Book/published by arrangement with
the author

PRINTING HISTORY
Berkley edition/June 1995

All rights reserved.
Copyright © 1995 by Leslie Rule.
This book may not be reproduced in whole or in part,
by mimeograph or any other means, without permission.
For information address: The Berkley Publishing Group,
200 Madison Avenue, New York, New York 10016.

ISBN: 0-425-14777-0

BERKLEY®
Berkley Books are published by The Berkley Publishing Group,
200 Madison Avenue, New York, New York 10016.
BERKLEY and the "B" design
are trademarks belonging to Berkley Publishing Corporation

PRINTED IN THE UNITED STATES OF AMERICA

10 9 8 7 6 5 4 3 2 1

1

SOMETIMES I WISHED I'D NEVER FOUND RITA'S diary. If I'd known all the trouble it would cause, I would have left it in its hiding place. But how could I have known that little musty book with its yellowing pages and rusty keyhole would get me involved in a *murder?*

My neighbor Suki was with me when I found the diary. We were poking around the attic of my family's old, rambling house.

It was built way back in 1870 and was actually made from real wood. That's rare here in Puget Sound. The old blind man who lived across the street said they stopped using wood to build houses around 2035 because of the tree shortage.

Suki's house was made from fiberglass and never needed to be painted like our funky old house did.

"Ick! A spider!" Suki suddenly shrieked. It skittered across the dusty floor on its thick, feathery legs and disappeared into a crack in the attic wall.

"It won't hurt you," I said. "We're used to spiders here. This house isn't airtight like yours. There are lots of places for bugs to get in."

She shuddered, her shoulders rising so they touched the ends of her limp blond hair. "Let's go back downstairs to your room where there aren't as many bugs."

"Go ahead," I said, and was relieved when she didn't. Last time she was alone in my room, I think she filched my new tube of strawberry lip tinter.

Suki had acted like my shadow ever since we'd moved to Banbury Bay in July when Mom inherited Great-aunt Ashley's old house. Just because Suki lived down the beach from us, and my father worked with her uncle at Twin-Star Labs, she acted as if we should be automatic best friends. I don't mean to sound cruel, but I preferred not to spend so much time with her. Suki was clingy and insecure and scared all the boys away with her mousey personality. If she didn't stop hanging around me, I'd never fit in at Banbury High.

At my old school in Salem, Oregon, I'd always been kind of an outsider. I was branded a rebel in the second grade—all because of a misunderstanding in the midst of one rainy afternoon. The stigma stayed with me forever. Or at least until we moved to Banbury Bay.

Sometimes when I looked back on that strange day in Salem, I got goose bumps. I couldn't explain what happened, and all these years later I still wondered. *I don't want to think about that. That is behind me now!*

I saw our move to Banbury Bay as a chance to start a new life, with new friends. But I knew I couldn't spend every waking moment with Suki unless I wanted to be labeled a total spard. It's a hard, cold fact that the crowd you hang with influences how people view you.

"This old house of yours really gives me the creeps, Jenna," Suki said. "Your attic is probably full of rats. Let's get out of here!"

"Go ahead. I want to see what's in this old trunk," I said, pulling a rusty bicycle off the dust-coated trunk in the corner.

"Probably more spiders."

I ignored her and popped open the lid. A thick, musty odor nearly knocked me over.

"It's just a bunch of old clothes," she said, peering over my shoulder.

It didn't look like anything too exciting, mostly faded blue jeans and ragged T-shirts. But I dug through the pile, partly because I was hoping Suki would get tired of watching me and leave. "Look at this!" I said. "It's a pair of old overalls. Somebody embroidered little hearts and peace signs on them. Do you think they belonged to a farmer?"

"There's something sticking out of the pocket!"

It was an old diary. A *very* old diary—its secrets long ago locked between the fading red vinyl covers. It would be easy to pick the lock. Someone had scribbled "Private" across the front cover. For a guilty instant, I considered tucking it back in the overalls. After all, what right did I have to read a stranger's secrets?

"Who did it belong to?" Suki's pale blue eyes sparked with sudden interest.

"Whoever it was is probably dead," I said. *Do the dead have a right to privacy?* I wondered. I turned the little book over and set it on the floor. "I could pick the lock if I had a piece of wire." The words were barely out of my mouth when the lock suddenly popped open—all by itself.

"*Weird!*" Suki whispered. "Maybe you've got ghosts up here!"

A shiver ran through me, but I laughed it off. "Would you relax? The lock was just worn-out. I must have jostled it when I set it down and it broke. That's all."

I opened the diary and a black-and-white photograph fluttered out. I stared into the familiar face and gasped.

2

"THAT'S *YOU!*" SUKI SAID. "HOW DID A PICTURE OF you get in that old diary? And who is that *cute* guy next to you?"

I couldn't answer her. All I could do was stare at the girl in the photograph. She had *my* face! The wide-spaced eyes. The button nose sprinkled with freckles. The slight overbite and too thin lips. Those were *my* features. But it wasn't a picture of me. I was certain.

I turned over the photograph and read: *Rita and Ben, Stones concert, Seattle Coliseum, 1970.* That picture was a *hundred* years old!

I finally found my voice. "It's not me. This picture was taken a century ago."

"She sure looks like you. She's even built like you, Jenna."

It was true. Rita had my long (but too skinny) legs and slim waist. She wore a flowered halter top and a faded pair of cutoff jeans embroidered with peace signs. Had Rita embroidered the overalls too? They must have been hers, I realized.

"Maybe that's you in another life," Suki suggested. "Maybe you were reincarnated."

"She's probably a relative of mine. We have the same genes. It's natural I'd inherit some of my family's characteristics," I said, trying to make sense of the eerie resemblance.

"It's not like she's your mom or something! She's a *distant* relative. If she were really born a hundred years ago, the genes would be watered down by now. You could inherit her nose or something, but not her *whole* face!"

Suki was right. It didn't make sense that I would look so much like a relative who was born a century before me. The fact is, I don't even resemble anyone in my immediate family. My parents are both short and round, while I am long and slender. I don't have my dad's prominent nose or my mom's startling violet eyes. My nose is one of those tiny upturned models and my eyes are an uninteresting gray. I'm different from my parents in so many ways, I can't even count them. I thought about this as I walked Suki home.

Her house is about a quarter of a mile from us. It's right on the water—so close the waves swish against her dining room window when it storms.

Our house is set back from the water, perched on a hill overlooking the beach. Our kitchen door opens onto a dirt path that snakes through a jungle of Scotch broom bushes and gradually slopes toward the rickety steps that lead to the beach.

"Do you think I should call him, Jenna?" Suki asked as we walked along the rocky shore. I knew who she meant. She had a thing for Kyle Mettley, a senior at our school. She chattered about him constantly.

"If you feel brave enough," I said without enthusiasm. My mind wasn't on her love life. I couldn't stop thinking about my resemblance to Rita, and my *lack* of resemblance to my family. What did it mean?

Everything about me was different from my parents. My dad is so logical. Science-minded. In fact, he *is* a scientist. He relies on calculations and carefully thought-out strategies to make decisions. I, on the other hand, operate on gut instinct. I make choices based on what I feel inside. I know I didn't get that trait from my mother. She's always second-guessing her decisions, and looks at me blankly when I tell her to follow her instincts.

Why was I so different from my parents?

"I wish Kyle was here with me now." Suki sighed. "This sunset is so romantic!"

The sun looked like a broken egg yolk oozing down the sky. It smeared the horizon in a beautiful, brilliant orange. It *was* romantic. I stopped to watch the sun dip behind the islands.

Rita must have watched the sunset from this very spot.

A hundred years ago.

Who was the good-looking guy in the photo with her? *Ben.* Did he and Rita sit on a log and kiss as the waves reflected the magnificent hues of the sky?

The answer might be here, I thought, and patted my jacket pocket where I'd tucked the diary. Suddenly, I couldn't wait to get home and read it. I'd felt funny about looking at it in front of Suki. A diary is such a personal thing. I didn't want her reading Rita's private thoughts. Rita was *my* relative. I'd inherited her face, so maybe we were alike in other ways too. It seemed right for *me* to know her secrets.

"Maybe I should write him a note," Suki interrupted my thoughts. "What do you think, Jenna?"

I didn't want to give her my opinion. Big, handsome Kyle with his impish green eyes and wheat-blond hair would surely laugh at her behind her back—or maybe even to her face—if she wrote him a note proclaiming her feelings. Kyle Mettley was not exactly known for his sensitivity.

He was a track star and his parents were wealthy. Kyle ruled the school and dated popular, pretty girls. Suki did not fall into that category. It's not that she was homely. She was slightly chubby, with a pleasant, even-featured face; she would have probably looked pretty good if she had a make-over. But she lacked *sparkle.* Her eyes were desperate and her smile nervous. And I felt drained whenever I spent time with her.

"Should I, Jenna? Should I write him a note?"

"I think you're jumping way ahead of yourself, Suki."

"You're right." She sounded relieved. "I should let him make the first move."

Of course he never would. I knew it and she knew it too. Kyle was a fantasy for her. He was simply someone to daydream about. Frankly, I was tired of hearing about him. I was tired of being her sounding board. I'd offered to walk her home only because I was afraid Mom would ask her to stay for dinner if she hung around any longer. Mom, a kindergarten teacher, was in the habit of fussing over her students and for some strange reason she fussed over Suki too.

"Come on in," Suki said, as we reached her dome-shaped house. It was tucked into a dent in the hillside and protected from the encroaching tide by a twelve-foot concrete bulkhead. "Uncle Terry wants to talk to you."

"Why?" I asked, startled. I glanced up and saw him watching us from one of the bubble-shaped windows. Another face appeared beside him as he gestured toward me.

"Why is he pointing at me?" A sudden prickle of warning ran through me. I was uneasy, but didn't know why.

A moment later I found myself in her living room as seven adults I'd never met before peered at me intently over their cocktails.

"Nice to meet you, Jenna," Suki's uncle said, and shook my hand, squeezing so tightly I though he'd break a bone. He was strong for such a skinny man. He reminded me of a skeleton coated in a thin layer of flesh. His dark eyes seemed to pierce right through me. "I'm Terry Grady, and these are some of my associates at Twin-Star Labs. They work with your father too."

I nodded politely at the other scientists, immediately forgetting their names as Dr. Grady introduced them. Nobody else got up to shake my hand. They remained seated on the plush pink sofa that curled around the length of the curved wall.

"So this is Jenna," a smooth-faced woman said a little too brightly. She leaned forward, her shiny red lips stretched into a phony smile. "We've heard a lot about you."

From who? I wondered. *Dad?* He'd never been the type to carry my photo in his wallet or display it on his desk. I couldn't imagine him actually talking about me to people at work. I didn't think he was even *interested* in me. My father and I have never been close.

"How would you like to earn some extra cash, Jenna?" Dr. Grady asked.

"Sure!" I said, a bit too enthusiastically. The scientists laughed, and I smiled self-consciously. I wished they'd stop staring at me like I was one of their specimens!

"We're doing a special study and we need teenagers to participate. We're starting this Saturday."

"What do I need to do?" I asked.

"Take a few tests. We're just testing a theory. Suki is going to participate, and she's suggested names of a few of your classmates."

I glanced at Suki, who was grinning broadly. *Great,* I thought. *Now I'll be stuck with her every Saturday!*

"I'll ask my parents," I said.

"We've already cleared it with your father. Now we need a commitment from you," he said. "Once we start, we can't have any dropouts or it will skew the results and we'll have to start all over. Can we count on you, Jenna?"

"Sure," I said, squirming slightly under his steady gaze.

"Come on," Suki said and pulled on my arm. "I want to show you something in my room."

When I stepped into her large, round bedroom, I gasped. Her walls were a brilliant, fiery orange—so bright they hurt my eyes.

"Like it?" she asked eagerly.

"Do you want my honest opinion?"

She sighed. "Maybe it is too much," she conceded. "I'll tone it down." She turned a dial by her door, and the orange walls flickered a moment before settling into a mellow tangerine shade.

My home in Salem had also had "Change-a-Walls"—walls made from sheets of Plexiglas with colored liquid trapped inside. With a flick of a switch, I could change the color and mood of my room instantly. I favored soft shades of lavender and baby blue. Sometimes I'd program in a gentle pattern for a wallpaper effect. Suki went for crazy shades and wild designs that almost always gave me a headache. Or maybe it was *Suki* who gave me a headache.

"I've got stuff to do at home," I told her, and she

tagged after me as I tried to slip past the living room where the scientists were engrossed in an animated discussion. They fell silent when they saw me. Had they been talking about *me?*

"Can you join us for dinner, Jenna?" Dr. Grady asked.

I insisted I had to get back to do my homework. (I couldn't imagine trying to digest food with all of them scrutinizing me!)

Suki followed me out onto the deck, reluctant to see me go. "Why don't you stay for dinner? That geography report isn't due until Monday." Her blue eyes shined anxiously. She was as eager as a puppy dog. You'd think she'd never had a friend before!

"Thanks, but I really have to get home."

"Wait just a minute. I'm going to run in and get the list of kids Uncle Terry scheduled to take the tests with us. He was supposed to call and hire them this afternoon, and I'm dying to see if they agreed to it. I hope he called the ones I asked him to. You won't believe it when you see who they are!"

She scurried inside and I leaned on the railing of the Gradys' deck and stared at the horizon. The sunset had deepened to purple, and the beach was cloaked in shadows. Dr. Grady poked his head out the door. "It's getting dark. I'll drive you home," he said, his scraggly eyebrows drawing together in concern.

I waved him away. "I walk fast. I'll be home before it's completely dark. Tell Suki I'll phone her," I called over my shoulder, hurrying down the steps toward the beach. The idea of being alone with him filled me with inexplicable dread. Something about him made my skin creep!

I lied to Dr. Grady. I had no intention of walking fast. I strolled slowly, inhaling the pungent, salty air and savoring the peaceful moments alone. The only sound was the gentle slapping of the waves. It felt good to get away from Suki's constant chatter.

Halfway home, my finger-watch phone beeped. Suki's face—in 3-D—appeared on my watch face. *Now what does she want?*

"Jenna, are you there?" Suki called. "Can you hear me?"

For a moment, I felt as if a miniature Suki face was growing from my finger—like an annoying planter's wart that refused to fall off. I turned off the finger-phone and her image vanished. Then I settled in on one of the huge logs a storm had washed ashore and opened Rita's diary. The light had nearly faded away so I read by my key ring flashlight.

March 3, 1970

Dear Diary,

I never should have listened to April! She told me I should "play hard to get!" She said Ben would lose interest if I didn't "act aloof" once in a while. She said—AND I QUOTE—"Men like a little mystery."

Well, I took April's advice. And I'd give anything if I hadn't. While I was busy being aloof, some tramp got her claws into the love of my life!

Why did I listen to April? She's never even had a boyfriend and has only been on three dates, and they were only with that skinny guy who bags groceries—

Marvin Fudsomething-or-other. Does that make her an expert????? I think not!

Maybe April WANTED to break me and Ben up because Shane doesn't want to date her. (Shane Murdock is Ben's best friend and he's gorgeous—though not as gorgeous as Ben.)

I guess I shouldn't be mad at April, but I have to blame someone. It hurts so bad. For the first time in my life, I'm really in love. I know I've said it before, but it was NEVER like this. Oh, Diary, I know I haven't told you anything about Ben. And I know I promised to write my every thought in you. But I've been so busy since I met him, I haven't had time. Now, as my tears fall on your pages, smearing the ink, I'll try to fill you in on the last weeks.

Diary, it started with his eyes. Ben has these really far-out eyes. They're the same shade of blue as a faded pair of jeans. And when he looks at me, I feel like he's looking into my soul. I know that sounds corny but—oh! Someone's knocking at the door. Maybe it's Ben!

I'm back, Diary. It wasn't Ben. No one was at the door. That's kind of scary, because I'm here alone. Mom's at her Yoga class and Dad's giving a guitar lesson. Jim is probably out raising hell on his bicycle with all the other eleven-year-old brats in the neighborhood. So when I answered the door and didn't see anybody, I slammed it fast. I kind of had the feeling someone was hiding in the bushes! I went around the house and locked all the windows, just in case. Lately

I've had this really weird feeling that someone's watching me!

A sudden sharp crack interrupted Rita's words. I nearly dropped the diary as I turned quickly toward the noise. It sounded like a twig snapping under a foot. But I couldn't see anyone. Immersed in Rita's world, I hadn't noticed the night creep in. The logs were shapeless shadows blending with the beach, and the water had turned black.

"Who is it? Who's there?" I called out tentatively. "Suki, is that you?" It would be exactly like her to follow me home when I'd just gotten rid of her. The pest!

Only the waves answered me, their rhythmic whispers caressing the sand. I aimed my flashlight in the direction the noise had come from—or rather where it seemed to have come from. On the water sound plays tricks.

The faint beam of my flashlight moved over the logs. I held my breath, half expecting to see a figure perched on a log, staring back at me. No one was there.

Someone could have been hiding behind a log. But I wasn't about to investigate! I stuffed the diary back in my pocket and headed toward home, this time walking briskly.

The distinct sound of footsteps crunching on rocks came behind me. *Someone is following me!*

My heartbeat thudded in my ears as I began to run. I bounded forward and my feet slid across the slippery, seaweed-coated rocks. Stumbling, I fell to my knees. Barnacles sharp as razors scraped the palms of my hands as I scrambled to my feet.

Adrenaline coursed through me, fueling me with a surge of energy that kept my legs pumping. I nearly flew over the beach, kicking unseen sticks and sea whips out of my path, running for my life.

I rounded the bend and was greeted by a ferocious bark. Relief flooded through me. It was old Mr. Edwards and his seeing-eye dog, Jake, a gangly German shepherd.

"Who's there?" Mr. Edwards yelled.

I skidded to a stop, gasping for breath. "It's me, Mr. Edwards! It's Jenna. Someone was following me!"

"Don't worry. Jake will take care of them," he said. "You can walk with us. We wander down here every night so Jake can do his business. That way I don't have to clean up after him. The tide comes in and does it for me."

I fell into step beside them. He was a small, bent man with a powerful voice. It was full and warm and filled the night. His chatter spun around me like a protective wall. Normally he bored me, but tonight I felt safe listening to him.

Jake suddenly bounded ahead, his leash trailing behind him. I wondered if I should offer Mr. Edwards my arm. But he was doing better than I was. While I tripped along the dark beach, he walked confidently, as if he sensed each protruding rock or washed up tennis shoe. Maybe his shoes were equipped with the radar device some seeing-impaired people use to detect obstacles. I wondered why he hadn't had his vision restored through surgery.

As if reading my mind, he said, "I might have had the surgery if I'd still been young. But Dr. Avery's discovery wasn't made until I was such an old goat I figured I'd kick the bucket any day."

"But sight restoration was discovered over twenty years ago!"

He chuckled. "I guess I was wrong. I'm still here. And I kind of like it in my dark little world. You want to try it?"

"What?"

"Close your eyes," he urged. "You've been tripping all over the beach. Close your eyes and see with your mind."

Obediently, I shut my eyes.

"See your path with your mind. I know you can do it. You won't trip."

The insides of my eyelids were red-black and I tried to see through them, picturing the course before me. But I saw only a black void, and imagined myself falling into it. Spinning downward into nothingness. It was the wrong thing to picture. The beach seemed to sway beneath my feet. I fought a wave of dizziness, tempted to peek.

"Don't try so hard. Relax. See with your mind. You can do it." His voice was hypnotic.

I drew a deep breath of cool, salty air and exhaled slowly. The tension slid from my muscles and I began to relax. He was right. I strolled easily beside him, no longer tripping as my feet carried me along.

In this dark world, the waves seemed louder. Thunderous. They smashed against the sand. As a breeze brushed my cheek, I tasted the air. Sharp and salty and slightly fishy, it slipped across my tongue and instantly evaporated. Like a new pungent flavor of cotton candy—there and gone before you could sink your teeth into it.

"I see a lot," Mr. Edwards said. "Some think I'm a crazy old man. But I *do* see. The lights went out for me so long ago, you'd think I wouldn't remember. I was just a boy."

"What happened?"

"An accident. A firecracker blew up in my face. Wiped out my sight. I guess I was pretty ugly," he said matter-of-factly. "The scars were bad. My mom couldn't stand to look at me. Of course I couldn't see her, but I sensed it when she turned away in disgust."

"That's awful!" I gasped.

"Don't feel sorry for me, Jenna. It was a long time ago. I wasted a few years feeling sorry for myself, and then I got on with life. I didn't let it make me bitter. I probably wouldn't be here now if I had. Remember that. Never become bitter. That's my advice to you."

"Sounds like good advice," I said politely.

"May I give you another piece of advice, young lady?"

"Sure."

"Don't walk on the beach after dark anymore. It's not safe for you. Did you know a girl was murdered here?"

3

WHEN I OPENED MY MOUTH TO REPLY, ONLY A scream came out because I suddenly found myself flying through the air. I had tripped on a piece of driftwood. My eyes popped open as I threw my hands out to catch myself. My right hand landed on a piece of broken glass as I hit the ground. The glass sliced through my palm and blood gushed out. "Oh!" I cried as the wound instantly began to sting.

"You hurt?"

"I cut myself!"

"Ouch," he said sympathetically. "When that salt water gets into a cut it really stings. We're almost to my house. I can wash that out for you and put a bandage on it."

"No thanks. It's not that bad. We've got bandages."

So much for "seeing my path," I thought. *I never should have listened to that crazy old man!*

"Remember my advice, Jenna!" Mr. Edwards called after me as I scrambled up the path. My house loomed before me, the windows on the first floor shining brightly. Mom hadn't bothered to pull the shades. I paused for an instant, imagining the house a hundred years before. It was easy to picture. Years ago, when Aunt Ashley first moved here, Banbury House had been declared a historic landmark. Remodeling was prohibited. The surrounding town might have changed, but the house remained the same.

Banbury House was all peaks and balconies and gingerbread lace. The roof rose to such a sharp point it seemed to jab at the sky, threatening to rip a hole in the night's clouds. It was painted canary-yellow and glowed in the moonlight.

Inside the wood floors gleamed—a beautiful (but creaky) feature my mother loved. Two twisting staircases and countless nooks gave the house a mysterious feel, as if someone could hide there for days and you'd never guess.

Suddenly, I knew. *Rita lived here.* She *must* have! Why else would her diary be in Banbury House! Which room was hers? My eyes swept up the side of the house to my room on the third story. I'd left the bedside lamp on, and the window glowed faintly, spilling light onto the maple tree branch that stretched beneath it. Mom had papered my room in an old-fash-ioned rose pattern that supposedly matched the original wallpaper. It was lacy and feminine. Definitely a girl's room.

Had it once been *Rita's* room?

I stared at the window. Had she been in that room—*my room*—when she wrote that someone was watching her? Had someone stood here in this very spot, staring at the house? *Staring at Rita?*

I shivered at the thought. The bright lights in our kitchen illuminated my parents in vivid detail as I watched them from outside. Dad was leaning against the counter, his stocky arms folded across his chest. The bald crown of his head glinted under the fluorescent lights, as his head bobbed up and down. His whole head always moved when he talked.

He must have said something funny because Mom was laughing. Her thick black hair fell into her eyes, and she brushed it aside and playfully punched him in the arm, oblivious to the fact that someone was standing outside peering in at her. Never mind it was *me!* *Anyone* could stand outside and stare in at us, and we wouldn't even know!

I felt a prickle of fear, remembering the footsteps on the beach. If someone *had* followed me, they might still be out there, lurking in the bushes!

My parents' jaws dropped when I charged through the kitchen door. I followed their eyes and saw the blood dripping off my hand.

"Oh my God!" Mom cried. "What happened?"

"It's not as bad as it looks," I said. "Did you know a girl was murdered on the beach?" It was the wrong thing to say. She immediately assumed someone had just been killed and *I* had narrowly escaped the same fate.

I set her straight as she cleaned my wound. "I wouldn't believe everything that crazy old man tells you, Jenna. He's quite elderly—over a hundred years old. Most likely his mind is going. I haven't heard about a murder."

"But we just moved here. It wouldn't have gotten much coverage in the news in Salem," I pointed out.

"Aunt Ashley would have phoned us if someone had been murdered. The only murder I ever heard about around here happened years ago. And it wasn't a girl."

"That's right," Dad said as he poured himself a cup of coffee. "About twenty years ago a fisherman snagged his line on a skeleton in Crab Cave. The thing had been down there for years. It had a bullet through its skull. The police never figured out who it was, but they could tell it was a male around forty without teeth."

"That's probably what Mr. Edwards was thinking of," Mom added as Dad disappeared into his study.

"He didn't mention any cave," I said. "He said a *girl*. He said she was killed on the *beach*!"

"I'm sure he was mistaken. But Mr. Edwards is right about one thing. You shouldn't be running around after dark," she said, turning away to put a stack of dishes in the cupboard.

"Mom, do you know who Rita Mills was?"

For an instant my mother seemed to freeze. I couldn't see her face, because she was turned away from me.

Her shoulders tensed, drawing the fabric of her pink blouse taut against her back. She carefully pushed the stack of dishes onto the shelf and turned to face me. "I don't know a Rita," she said distractedly. "Is she a neighbor of ours?"

"I found her picture in the attic. I think she's one of your ancestors. Mom, she looks just like *me*!"

"How interesting. At least we know you look like someone in the family," she teased, and tugged on a strand of my hair.

"Seriously. Isn't it kind of weird I look so much like her?"

Before she could answer, the kitchen phone rang and a handsome face appeared on the large video screen. It was Kyle Mettley! I smoothed my hair back before I clicked the button so he could see me on his phone too.

"Hey," he said.

"Hey yourself," I answered, my heart thumping crazily. What was Kyle Mettley doing calling *me*?

"I heard we're both going to be working for Dr. Grady. I was wondering if you'd like a ride to the lab tomorrow."

So that's why Suki was so excited! She had asked her uncle to hire Kyle. I could see why she was so crazy about him. He had strong, masculine features and a dazzling smile that lit up his sexy green eyes.

"Sure. I could use a ride," I said, trying to sound casual.

"Marla Rindler, Josey Bells, Mike Willoby, and Karen Stokes all got hired."

It was an exclusive bunch! Suki had asked her uncle to hire the most popular kids at school. She clearly saw this as her chance to join the golden group.

"Suki Grady is going to be there too," I said.

"She's Grady's niece," he said. "He *had* to ask her. There's always one spard at every party."

"Oh," I teased. "So you think this is going to be a party? I thought it was *work*!"

"It's a party if *I'm* there," he said cockily.

Just then the screen split as another call came through. Suki's face filled the left half of the screen, and I felt a twinge of guilt at seeing her eyes shining so happily. She'd die if she knew Kyle had called her a spard.

"Sorry, Kyle. There's someone on the other line," I said, and put our audio connection on hold.

"Oh, Jenna! Where have you *been*?" Suki squealed. "I called you three times! Wait till you hear! Kyle is going to be at the lab tomorrow. Uncle Terry hired him to work with us!"

"That's great," I said. "I'm on the other line, can we talk about this tomorrow?"

What would she think if she knew her image was pressed against Kyle's on my phone's video screen? It was probably the closest she'd ever come to snuggling up to him.

"What do you think I should wear tomorrow?" she asked.

Kyle was fidgeting impatiently, obviously tired of being on hold.

"Wear your pink puff-suit. It looks really nice on you," I added kindly and punched the button so Kyle's gorgeous face filled the entire screen once again.

We flirted for another minute and then someone from the lab phoned for Dad, interrupting my call again.

I wanted to continue my conversation with Mom about the old photo, but Dad said she'd gone to bed with a headache. It was only 7 p.m. I had the oddest feeling she was avoiding me. She had seemed almost frightened when asked about my resemblance to Rita. And there was no mistaking the relief on her face when Kyle's call interrupted our talk.

Was it my imagination, or was my mother hiding something from me?

4

UPSTAIRS IN MY ROOM I SAT BY MY ANTIQUE dresser, held Rita's photograph next to my face, and stared into the mirror. I was struck again by the resemblance. She was laughing, so I laughed too. Dimples—just like hers—appeared in my cheeks. My eyes squinted and became the same half-moons as Rita's. Were hers the same ocean-sky gray? The black-and-white photograph couldn't tell me.

"I wish I knew you, Rita," I whispered. I went to my window, an old-fashioned bay window complete with a seat, and gazed into the night. The moon was high and cast a silvery path across the black water. I leaned against a fat cushion and opened Rita's diary.

I first noticed Benjamin Grand in History class. He sits across the aisle from me and always has something wonderfully rebellious to say to Mr. Frink. We all hate Mr. Frink because he's boring and cruel—the worst possible traits in a teacher!

Anyway, Mr. Frink was picking on Sue Mitchell. She's this slow girl who always forgets to bring her book to class. (I think it's because she can't remember her locker combination.) Mr. Frink really loves to make her squirm. He always makes her stand up and give the class a complete report on how she managed to not bring her book. She gets really embarrassed and her face turns bright pink, and everyone knows she's trying really hard not to cry. Well, right in the middle of this harassment, Ben interrupted! He said, "Mr. Frink, I forgot my book too. Would you like me to explain to the class how this terrible oversight happened?"

He was being sarcastic, of course, so everyone laughed—except Mr. Frink. (Mr. Frink hates Ben because he has long hair.) So then Ben launched into this HILARIOUS long story that didn't have anything to do with his history book. Finally Mr. Frink (who was turning as pink as Sue) barked, "Would you get to the point, Mr. Grand?" But then the bell rang and everybody got up and charged out the door!

I thought it was really nice of Ben to get Sue off the hook like that. I smiled at him as we headed down the hall, and we ended up walking together to the cafeteria. I fell in love with him over lunch. As I mentioned earlier, it was Ben's eyes that did me in. They are fringed with long, black lashes, and so blue they're nearly white—like bleached-out denim. But it's not the color of his eyes or his eyelashes that makes them so *beautiful. It's what's inside those eyes. Does that make sense?*

It was as if she was talking directly to me. So I answered her. "Yes, Rita, it *does* make sense! I wish I could meet someone like your Ben."

And then I remembered he broke her heart! The ink was slightly smeared, so I knew she was still crying as she wrote. I felt for her. *Maybe they'll get back together,* I thought and was tempted to flip to the end of the diary to see what had happened. Instead, I kept reading.

We ate lunch together, but I couldn't taste my food. I honestly don't know if I ate anything. All I could think of was Ben—although I was distracted by April making faces at me from the next table. She kept raising her eyebrows and winking at me, as if to say, "Right on!" It was so embarrassing, I could have killed her! Luckily, I don't think Ben noticed.

It started with that lunch, and soon it was every lunch. Each afternoon after school, Ben gave me a ride home in his big clunky car and we'd sit on the beach and talk for hours or hang out at my house listening to my Beatles albums.

The first time Ben kissed me, we were on the beach. Our lips fit together as if they were designed to kiss each other. I snuggled against his jean jacket and got lost in the wonderful warm circle of his arms. I would have stayed that way forever, but Jim and his friend Chuck were spying on us from the cliff above. They threw globs of wet seaweed on us and some of it slid down the back of my shirt! Why did God invent little brothers?

Well, diary, I'm not going to tell you about every kiss. There were so many over the last weeks. They were the most blissful weeks of my life. But then April told me I should have some kind of a commitment from Ben. She said that if I was always available to spend time with him, he would lose interest. You see, Ben went camping with his friend Shane Murdock without telling me first. He left me hanging with no plans for the weekend! April slept over Saturday night, and when I griped about Ben's camping trip, she told me to "play hard to get.""

When I saw Ben on Monday I acted totally bored and disinterested. He looked shocked at first and then he got irritated. I ate lunch with April and he ate with his friends. We ended up not talking all week.

I was hoping we'd make up on Friday. There was a kegger on the beach—that's Ben's favorite kind of party because he loves beer. But Ben didn't ask me, so April and I went together. (We told Mom we were going to the movies.) When I saw Ben my heart stopped for a moment! He was sitting on a log with a bunch of his friends. But he turned away from me and drank his beer. I got a big cup of beer (which I hate!) and kind of sipped on it, waiting around for Ben to look my way.

When I looked up, a blonde I'd never seen before came out of nowhere and swooped down on Ben! I was about twenty yards from them so I couldn't see her clearly. But I did notice the tight sweater she had on. She stood next to him, one hand on her hip, and the other on Ben's shoulder! I was fuming!

April whispered, "You don't need him, Rita." But she was wrong. I do need him! Ben and "Tight Sweater" walked down the beach together and disappeared around the bend. Tears started to bubble up and sting my eyes. But it would have been humiliating to cry in front of people because they'd know Ben had hurt me. So I just started guzzling beer! At first I had a hard time choking it down. It's so bitter! But my second and third beer went down easier.

Well, Diary, April says I made an ass of myself. I started laughing too loud and flirting with all of Ben's friends. Shane tried to get me to sit down and eat some potato chips. (That was the only food left.) I think he was worried I was going to do something crazy. He was right. I set off down the beach to find Ben and that tramp!

April followed me, egging me on. "You tell him, Rita," she said. "Tell him he can't treat you like this."

She didn't know it, but it wasn't Ben I was going to tell off. I was looking for "Tight Sweater," and when I found her I was going to let her have it!

I rounded the bend and came face-to-face with her. It was pretty dark by then, so I couldn't see her very well. But I could tell she was shocked because her mouth popped open and she turned away.

"Hey, chick!" I said, sounding tougher than I knew I could. "Where's Ben?"

She didn't answer me, so I shouted, "Where's Ben?"

"What's it to you?" she said all bitchy-like. Well, there was something in her tone that really made me mad. I grabbed her arm and swung her around to face me. But she wouldn't look at me. She kept turning her face away. Finally, she said, "Ben doesn't care about you!"

That did it. I hauled off and smacked her across the face. I can still hear the sound it made (a very satisfying crack) as my open palm crashed against her cheek. She cried out and lurched into the bushes. By then a crowd had gathered. And I think the guys were disappointed that she didn't fight back. (It was the most exciting thing that happened at that party all night.)

Diary, I hope you're not too shocked by my violence. It shocked me a little. Yet, it also made me feel cleansed.

I don't know what happened to Ben that night. April and I got home way after the movie was supposed to have ended. I threw up in the front yard. Mom came out and caught me and knew I was drunk and that I'd lied about the movie. So now I'm grounded!

I wanted to keep reading, but the lights flickered and went out. There are some real drawbacks to living in an old house with old-fashioned electricity and antiquated plumbing! I climbed into bed and fell asleep, dreaming of Rita.

In the morning I sat at my maple dresser and pulled a brush through my long, wavy brown hair. When I fished in the drawer for my makeup, I couldn't find my Midnight Mist eyelid shadower. *Suki!* She'd managed to steal from me again.

I blinked. There, next to my comb, was my strawberry lip tinter—the lip tinter Suki had stolen when she visited last week. I was positive it hadn't been there yesterday. Suki was *really* strange. She'd stolen my lip tinter, returned it, and taken my eyelid shadower!

No wonder she didn't have any friends.

Mom was still acting funny at breakfast, and it wasn't because I asked more questions about Rita. I deliberately avoided the subject. I'd decided to find out about Rita without her help.

Mom was upset because of my new job. "I don't think it's a good idea for you to work," she said. "You need to concentrate on your studies."

"It's not really work. Dr. Grady just wants me to take some tests. It's only on Saturdays."

"Saturdays should be fun. You take tests at school all week," she said. It was the first time she'd been concerned about my having fun on Saturdays. In fact, she usually put me to work cleaning the house. Her sudden concern for my "fun" was puzzling.

"Dr. Grady is counting on Jenna," Dad said through a mouthful of cereal. "She made a commitment to him."

It surprised me that he intervened on my behalf. He usually stayed out of my arguments with Mom. My parents were behaving totally out of character!

Mom glowered at Dad, her eyes an odd mixture of

anger and worry. Before she could protest anymore, Kyle honked his horn and I dashed outside.

When we walked into Twin-Star Labs, the first thing I saw was Suki, sitting alone in the reception area. She dropped the magazine she was reading when she saw me with Kyle.

He gripped my elbow and steered me to the reception desk. "We're here to see Dr. Grady," he told the plump receptionist.

"Hello, Kyle!" she greeted him. "We haven't seen you in a while. Have a seat. Dr. Grady will be with you in a moment."

I sat on the couch across from Suki. Kyle plopped down next to me, so close his thigh pressed against mine, sending a shiver of excitement through me. I smiled sheepishly at Suki. Her eyes were wide with astonishment.

I flushed guiltily, then felt a flash of anger. How dare she make me feel guilty? She didn't own Kyle. It wasn't as if I'd stolen her boyfriend. *She* was the one stealing things.

"You guys are the first ones here," she said, sounding much too cheerful. "Uncle Terry had to get here early and I've been really bored sitting and waiting for everyone."

"Is that right?" Kyle said distractedly, not bothering to look at her. She didn't seem to notice and nodded happily, thrilled he'd spoken to her.

"The others should arrive soon, don't you think?" she gushed, looking expectantly at me.

Her enthusiasm sounded so *desperate*. I wished I could find a nice way to tell her that. "I love your puff-suit," I said, trying to put her at ease. "Pink looks great on you."

"Want to listen to music?" Kyle asked, handing me a Tune-Chip. "I programmed it with extra drums."

I tucked the tiny chip in my ear, clipping the regulator to my earlobe as Kyle did the same with another chip. He bobbed his head and tapped his foot, enjoying the beat only he could hear.

It was strange how music had changed since Rita's time when kids shared musical experiences—listening to songs on record players or at concerts with thousands of other people. Everyone heard the exact same tunes. Now, teenagers programmed Tune-Chips with their favorite instruments. The beat of the music adjusted to the individual's heartbeat, breathing, and stress level.

As I listened to the synthesized computer voice, I remembered Mom telling me that at one time authorities feared teenagers were negatively influenced by messages in music. The Tune-Chip was designed to end that concern. It sensed distress levels in individuals and adjusted its beat so the listener relaxed.

Adults still went to concerts, but most teens—unless they were complete spards—preferred Tune-Chips.

I pulled out my chip as the door flew open and Josey and Marla burst in, giggling and tossing their shiny blond hair. Mike and Karen arrived shortly, and

I soon found myself in the midst of a group of the most popular kids in school.

"Marla, that's a *frazzin* puff-suit!" Suki exclaimed.

Marla looked startled, as if unsure who Suki was. "Thanks," she mumbled, turning away to flirt with Mike.

"Wait till you guys see what my uncle wants you to do," Suki butted in. "It's a really weird experiment!"

Everyone ignored her. She clearly was not welcome to join in. Realizing this, she tried to draw me into a conversation. "Jenna, do you want to go to the mall later?" she asked. "There's a new program I want to try at the virtual reality arcade."

"That sounds like fun," I said. "But I've got lots to do today. Maybe next week."

From the corner of my eye, I saw the flash of hurt in her eyes. For an instant I felt a pang. I hardened myself to it. She should be making other friends. I was willing to hang out with her sometimes, but I saw no reason for us to be joined at the hip like a pair of Siamese twins.

This was *my* chance to finally belong to the right group, and I'd never get a chance to make friends if I committed every moment of my life to Suki.

"You're the new girl who lives in Banbury House, aren't you?" Marla asked, smiling.

"Yeah," I said. "It's like living in a museum some-times. The house is a historic landmark, so the city makes us have an open house once a month. We have to give tours!"

"How annoying!" Marla said. "I'd hate to have to clean my room that often."

"I just shove everything under my bed," I admitted.

"It's kind of a spooky old house," Marla said. "Is it haunted?"

"I hope not." I laughed. "But you're right about it being scary. Especially after last night when I heard a girl got murdered on the beach."

Suddenly all eyes were upon me. Even the receptionist looked up, her mouth dropping open. Then they were all talking at once, asking questions I had no answers to. "Who was it? When did it happen?"

"I don't know," I said. "I was hoping you guys could tell me."

"Where did you hear this?" Kyle asked, narrowing his eyes skeptically.

"Probably from Old Man Edwards!" Suki blurted. "He's got brain-drag. He's always rambling on about stuff like that. You can't believe a word he says."

A warm flush crept up my neck. Embarrassed, I admitted I'd heard about the murder from him.

A smug smile played on Suki's lips when everyone laughed. Laughed at *me*. She seemed pleased she'd made me look foolish!

"I like my girls gullible," Kyle said, patting my knee with an exaggerated lecherous wink.

"Knock it off, Kyle!" Marla squealed. "You're such a dirty old man!"

"Dirty *young* man," he said and stuck out his tongue, pretending to pant. I punched him in the arm, and found myself laughing along with everyone, relieved to realize they weren't laughing *at* me, they were laughing *with* me, as the old saying goes.

"I am *not* gullible!" I said. "I'm just new here. That's all."

"That's right," Marla defended me. "Jenna hasn't had a chance to sort out the crazies yet."

Suki was fading into the background, her moment of glory over. No one was listening to her anymore. Any sympathy I had for her had vanished when she'd deliberately tried to embarrass me in front of my new friends.

"Hey, Kyle," Marla said. "What are you doing here anyway? I thought your family owned this place. You don't need to work."

He stiffened, his leg suddenly rigid against mine. "You think I get a free ride?" His voice was sharp with irritation. "We own an interest in Twin-Star Labs, but that doesn't mean I can't pull my weight and go to work too."

Marla giggled nervously. "Hey, I didn't mean anything by it. It's just if my parents owned half the town, I wouldn't get up at seven in the morning. I'd sleep till noon and then spend the day lying back munching choco-mals and watching the maid pick up the wrappers."

Kyle laughed in spite of himself, but his voice was still edged with annoyance. "Choco-mals aren't on my diet. You forget I'm an athlete. And I *don't* have a personal maid."

"You poor deprived kid," Mike joked. He was Kyle's best buddy, a fellow track star with wavy red hair. Kyle seemed to relax as his friend ribbed him good-naturedly.

As I watched my new friends, my mind inexplicably flew back to Rita. What would she think of the way things had changed? Our outfits would certainly look strange to her eyes. Like Suki and me, most of the girls favored puff-suits—loose-fitting garments of Feather-Fabric that cinched at the waist and flared at the knees.

Feather-Fabric, copied from nature, regulated body temperatures by automatically loosening or tightening it fibers, allowing air to circulate or be trapped against the skin. The oily-like sheen was not only beautiful, it repelled rain or accidental spills.

Lots of guys had clothing made from Feather-Fabric, but the basic cut of their outfits hadn't changed much since Rita's time. I glanced at Kyle beside me. He looked great in a bold blue sweater and black Feather-Fabric slacks. I imagined him through Rita's eyes. Would she find him as attractive as Ben?

"What are you smiling about?" Kyle asked me.

I suddenly realized I was staring at him and grinning like an idiot. Flustered, I said, "I was just remembering something," and then I turned to Marla and offered her my Tune-Chip.

There wasn't much more time to socialize, because the receptionist soon hustled us down a long hallway where we were ushered into separate rooms. The rooms were small, stark cubicles not much bigger than bathrooms. I sat on one of the two straight-backed chairs facing a big glass tank with a strange-looking gadget inside.

"Glad to see you made it, Jenna," Dr. Grady said in his no-nonsense way as he entered with a young brunette woman in a lavender lab jacket. "This is Tarynn. She'll be recording the results," he said, as she took the seat beside me.

"As for you, Jenna," he continued, "I want you to watch the dice as they slide down this little shoot here." He pointed at the glass tank and turned a switch. Inside the tank, an automated scooper picked up a pair of dice and placed them at the top of the shoot. A moment later a lever swung out and knocked the dice down the shoot. They landed on the floor of the tank.

"That's all I have to do?" I asked. "Watch the dice fall?"

"Actually, I need you to do some concentrating too," he said. "I want you to try to make the dice fall a certain way. For instance, let's try to make them come up as sixes?"

He flipped the switch, and the scooper picked up the dice and placed them again at the top of the shoot. "Now, Jenna! *Concentrate*. Make them sixes!"

"*How?* Are there control buttons?" I asked, baffled.

"Use your mind," he urged. "Pretend you're gambling and you'll win a million dollars if they come up sixes."

It was a strange request, but I furrowed my brow and pictured the dice coming up sixes. When the lever bumped the dice, they slid clinking down the shaft and tumbled into the middle of the tank. A three and a two.

I glanced at Dr. Grady, surprised to see his face fall in disappointment. "Well. It will take some practice," he said.

"I don't understand," I said. "How can I control the dice without touching them?"

"We're doing a study on psychokinetic powers," Tarynn volunteered.

"Psycho-*what*?"

"Psychokinetics," Dr. Grady said. "Scientists have found that the human mind has the ability to affect objects without touching them. J. B. Rhine, a famous parapsychologist who lived in the twentieth century, conducted a study with dice with an apparatus similar to this."

I stared at him doubtfully.

"I know this sounds strange to you, Jenna. But several decades ago psychokinetic studies were quite common. Our conservative government of recent years, however, dramatically cut the budget for paranormal studies. That's probably why you haven't heard of psychokinesis. But there is evidence some people have a natural ability for this type of thing."

"We think you're one of them," Tarynn blurted, "because this ability is inherited."

"Inherited from *who*?" I asked, stunned. But Dr. Grady glared at Tarynn, his eyes hard and dark under those fierce, wild eyebrows. "We haven't much time," he said brusquely. "I've got to get the others started,

Jenna. Don't fill your head with the whys of what we're doing. Relax and concentrate on the dice."

But my mind was spinning. Why did they think *I* had mind powers? And what did she mean about this ability being inherited? Who did I inherit it from? *My parents?*

"What did you mean a minute ago?" I asked Tarynn when Dr. Grady left us alone.

"Never mind," she said, popping open the tiny computer on her wrist. "I really put my foot in it. I'll be lucky if he doesn't fire me."

"Just tell me. How come they think I have psycho-however-you-say-it?"

Her soft brown eyes darted around nervously. "I shouldn't have said anything. I need this job. I'm putting myself through school."

"I promise not to say anything. Please tell me."

"The walls have ears," she said, shifting uncomfortably.

Startled, I glanced at the stark white walls. My session was probably being videotaped. I couldn't see a camera, but Dad had mentioned that Twin-Star had camera lenses so small they could fit on the head of a pin.

Tarynn was pale, and her lower lip quivered like she was trying not to cry. She was really worried about losing her job. If Dr. Grady was my boss, I'd be upset too. He looked mean when he was mad! I decided to let it go and get to work.

"Concentrate on fours," Tarynn instructed as she hit the lever. *Four, four, four,* I thought, as I watched the dice roll down the shoot and tumble to a stop. A four and a three.

"Keep thinking fours," she said. For the next fifteen minutes, we repeated the process. The dice came up on fours sometimes, but also landed on every other possible combination.

"I don't think I have any powers," I told her. "This seems pretty random."

"We won't know until we tally the totals," she explained. "It's based on statistics. If a number comes up more often than average, that indicates a possible psychokinetic ability."

When she asked me to concentrate of fives, I decided to mentally keep track of how many fives I got. The first time down the shoot, the dice came up a pair of fives. And then a five and a three. And then two fives again. A four and a one. A five and a three. Two fours. Two fives. A five and a four.

"I'm doing good, aren't I?" I asked, excited.

"I think so," she said, her eyes shining as she entered the data into the computer.

I concentrated harder, visualizing the five black dots on the cube of white. Tarynn pushed a button, speeding up the process, so the dice seemed constantly in motion. Tumbling, rattling, sliding down the shoot. Two fives. A five and a four. A five and a six. Two fives. Two fives. Two fives.

"I'm doing it! *I'm* controlling the dice!" I cried. "I've got it, haven't I? Psycho-whatever abilities!"

"Psychokinetic abilities. PK for short."

Two fives. Two fives. A five and a six. A five and a one. Two fives. Two fives. Two fives.

"This is *incredible*," she whispered, her eyes lit in awe.

Two fives. Two fives. A six and a three. Two fives. A five and a four. Two fives. Two fives. Two fives.

"I can control things with my mind!" I said. "If I can make dice land on fives, I wonder what else I can do."

"Maybe you can make a paper clip disappear," she said. "Like your sister did." The instant the words escaped from her lips, Tarynn looked like she wanted to bite off her tongue.

I stared at her in shock. Either she had me confused with someone else, or I had a sister no one had told me about.

5

IF I HAVE A SISTER, WHERE IS SHE? I WONDERED, MY thoughts whirling. I sat in my window seat, watching the sunlight sparkle on the waves.

It was late afternoon and my mind was crammed with all that had happened in the lab. My parents were out, and I was anxiously waiting for them so I could grill them about what Tarynn had said.

My *sister*!

I'd always wanted a sister. Someone to trade secrets with. Someone to laugh with, to talk to. Someone to trade clothes with. Someone I could be completely myself with and sometimes get mad at and it wouldn't matter because we'd always make up because we were *sisters*.

A sister would understand me. Sisters, after all, are

alike. I wouldn't feel like such an alien in my own family if I had a sister.

I'd always felt cheated because my parents wouldn't—or *couldn't*—give me a sister.

In fact, when I was little I had an imaginary sister I called Cassandra. I used to talk to her and have tea parties with her before I started school. She caused me a lot of trouble in the second grade.

That was the year all my problems began. That's when the strange things occurred that caused my teacher to label me a troublemaker and my classmates to label me "weird."

I still couldn't explain what had happened. All I knew was that chaos had erupted around me in the classroom. Chairs fell over when no one but I was near enough to push them over. Books jumped off shelves. The trash can tipped over. An apple flew across the room and hit Bobbie Bloomingdale in the back of the head.

I can't explain it now, I thought. *And I couldn't explain it them.* So I had blamed it on Cassandra.

My imaginary sister.

For a while I actually believed I'd wished Cassandra into existence. *Someone* had to move those things, didn't they? So I decided Cassandra had thrown that apple at Bobbie. I hated him because he made fun of my freckles. Cassandra was simply sticking up for me.

Ms. Marmalton didn't believe me and sent me to the principal's office. No one believed that Cassandra had started the trouble. But I stuck to my story.

I remembered my mother's flushed face and worried eyes as she sat with me in the principal's office, crossing and uncrossing her legs. She'd stuck up for me, crisply informing the principal that "Jenna is a quiet child. She is not a troublemaker. Some other child must have thrown those things."

But afterward, when we were alone in the hallway, she had pulled me close and whispered in my ear, "Jenna, this must *never* happen again. Do you understand me? *Never!*"

"But I didn't do it! Cassandra did!"

She'd smiled weakly, her eyes pleading. "However it happened—whoever did it—it must never happen again. This will be our secret. Don't ever tell Dad or anyone else what occurred today."

I didn't *want* to tell anyone so I'd readily agreed to the secret. I didn't want Cassandra to get into trouble.

Of course, when I got older I knew there was no Cassandra. You don't *wish* a person into existence. But the fact remains, objects flew around that room on their own. And objects can't move by themselves—*unless* . . .

Suddenly, my mind was reeling. Maybe those objects *didn't* move on their own. Maybe I *had* moved them, the way I controlled the dice!

Excited, I rushed to my computer. My fingers typed in a command, and my computer's modem accessed the magazine files in Banbury Library. Within seconds my computer screen pulled up several articles on psychokinesis. After a moment of scanning I found what I was looking for:

Sometimes PK abilities appear to erupt from an individual's mind without that person's awareness. Furniture is overturned. Objects are hurled about rooms, lights turn on and off, and pounding vibrates the walls. Some parapsychologists have attributed the disturbance to poltergeists—ghosts believed to haunt places where children or adolescents are present. But research indicates that the disruption may actually be caused by a child's mind.

Dazed, I leaned back in the chair. Could I really move things with my mind? A shiver slithered up my neck. It was a frightening thought.

Yesterday I would have laughed off the possibility of mind over matter. But that was before I knew Twin-Star Labs was researching it. Researchers, like my father, were actually conducting experiments on it! And I knew they didn't waste time on anything that didn't have a scientific basis.

The scientists at Twin-Star Labs were logical and precise. I knew from watching my father work that they documented everything and rarely made mistakes. Was Tarynn mistaken about my having a sister? I didn't think so. She'd heard it from someone, maybe even read it in a file. *My* file!

It made me uneasy, thinking Twin-Star Labs had a file on me—on my *family.* Suddenly, the word "family" had a funny taste to it.

"Family." It tumbled off my tongue sounding inexplicably foreign. *Family.* You inherit things from your family. Things like hair color and height and nose shape.

And psychokinetic ability.

With a sudden, cold certainty, I knew the people I called "Mom" and "Dad" weren't really my parents. Somewhere, I had another set of parents—my *real* parents. And living with them, was my sister.

"Don't be ridiculous!" Mom said. "Of course you're not adopted!"

I'd confronted her before she made it through the front door. She stood framed in the doorway, her plump arms wrapped around a lumpy bag of groceries. She shook her head, laughing.

"Why don't I look like you?" I demanded.

"Genes are a funny thing, Jenna," she said, thrusting the groceries into my arms. "Here, help me with these. I've got three other bags in the car."

I shoved the groceries onto the counter and followed Mom out to our solar-mobile. "I don't look like Dad either!"

"Thank God!" she said, laughing some more. Nervous laughter.

"That's not funny, Mom. If I was adopted, I wish you'd just admit it! I know I have a sister!"

"Where did you hear *that*?" she said, sounding decidedly less amused.

"Somebody let it slip at the lab today," I explained. "She tried to act like it was a mistake—that she had me confused with someone else. But I knew she was lying."

"You have a rich imagination, dear. I swear to you,

you are *not* adopted. *I* gave birth to you! And I've got pictures of me looking like a barn to prove it."

"There are photos of you pregnant?" I asked as the wind seeped from my argument.

"Of course! They're on the computer with the rest of the family pictures. As soon as we put these groceries away, I'll show you so you'll stop this nonsense."

Mom was telling the truth. The photos were there in vivid color in our computer files. "See, that's me nine months pregnant with you," she said, gushing sentimentally as a picture of her in a polka-dot maternity dress appeared on the screen.

A warm wave of relief flowed through me. Mom was right. Sometimes my imagination got the better of me.

We sat before the computer, getting lost in the photos and family mementos. I'd always loved to draw, and sentimental Mom had saved all my artwork by programming it into the computer, even the silly scribblings from my preschool days!

I remembered how she'd exclaimed over my drawings—as only a mother could—and insisted on putting them on display, saying, "Jenna, you've got more talent in your little finger than I do in my whole body. I couldn't draw water from a well!" It was a corny joke, but she always looked so proud of me that I forgave her for it.

Our computer album held hundreds of photos of me.

"You were a beautiful baby," Mom sighed, as a

"moving photo" of me in my first bathing suit flickered across the screen. She turned up the volume so we could hear the babyish giggling as a one-year-old me happily splashed in the wading pool, then jumped out and ran dripping across the yard.

"Why didn't you have more babies, Mom?"

"I was forty when I met your father," she said wistfully. "It was a little late to start a big family."

"So I definitely *don't* have a sister?"

A tolerant smile inched across her round face. "I think I would know if I had other children," she said gently. "To the best of my recollection, I gave birth to only one."

"You're always making jokes. Did you or *didn't* you have another baby?"

"I only had you."

"What about Dad? Did *he* have other children? Do I have a half sister somewhere?"

"Your father has no other children."

Before I had a chance to quiz Mom about how I'd inherited my so-called psychokinetic abilities, the sudden shriek of a siren sent us running to the window. An ambulance whizzed past our house, lights whirling as it headed down our quiet street.

"Oh, no!" Mom cried. "There's been some kind of an accident!"

I followed her out onto our wide front porch. Neighbors popped from their houses, craning their necks toward the ambulance, which had parked at the bottom of the hill where the road met the beach.

"Do you know what happened, Ruby?" Mom called

out to the gray-haired woman who lived to the right of us.

"All I know is that somebody fell off Windy Cliff," our neighbor yelled back. "Some kid saw him fall from a distance. He ran up the hill and asked me to call the ambulance."

"Poor soul!" Mom said, her eyes wandering to the cliff that loomed above us. Our small neighborhood of scattered old houses sat on Banbury Hill, which sloped down toward the north and then rose into a monstrously steep hill known as Windy Cliff. Twice as high as Banbury Hill, Windy Cliff jutted out to the west, hundreds of feet above the rocky beach.

The cliff was too rugged to build on, but people liked to wander up there because of the view. It was hard to imagine anyone surviving a fall from Windy Cliff.

The ambulance crew quickly unloaded a stretcher and headed down the beach. Several neighborhood kids sped down the road on their electric skates and swarmed around the ambulance, waiting to see what the crew would bring back.

"Should we go down and see what happened?" I asked Mom.

"Let's wait here," she said. "I don't like to gawk at accidents. If there was something we could do to help, that would be one thing. The ambulance attendants have it under control. We'd just be in the way."

We watched from our porch, and a few minutes later the crew returned, carrying a stretcher. A large brown dog raced frantically around them, barking wildly.

"That's Jake!" I cried. "That's Mr. Edwards's dog! Oh, Mom! Do you think it's Mr. Edwards?"

"It must be," she whispered. "Poor old man."

"I-I was just talking to him last night," I said, as hot tears spilled down my cheeks. "I can't believe it."

Most of our neighbors had gathered into a somber group on the edge of Ruby's lawn. They shook their heads, voices dropped to a shocked murmur.

The form on the stretcher lay very still. It was completely covered by a stark white sheet. If that was Mr. Edwards under that sheet, he was dead.

6

"I SAW HIM FALL," KYLE TOLD US, HIS VOICE shaking. "I parked my car at the boat ramp at View Point Park and walked down the beach. I was on my way to see you. I thought you might like to take a boat ride. I-I'd just come around the bend and I saw him falling through the air. He was screaming."

"How awful!" Mom gasped.

We were seated in the living room, on the lumpy antique couch Mom had reupholstered in "Victorian Ivy." Kyle gulped the glass of water Mom had given him when she saw how pale he looked. "I ran up the hill and saw your neighbor," he told us. "I yelled to her to call for help and then I ran back to the beach to see if I could do anything to help him. But he was dead."

"You did everything you could," Mom said gently. "No one could survive a fall like that."

"What was he doing up on the cliff?" I wondered aloud. "Most people go up there for the view. But Mr. Edwards can't—couldn't—see."

"He was a little senile," Mom reminded me. "A lot of things he did didn't make sense."

"I know." I sighed. "He thought he could see with his mind. He'd let Jake off his leash and walk by himself without a cane or anything. He must have walked right off the cliff!"

"It's a terrible way to go," Mom said. "But he had a good long life. He was well over a hundred."

"Yeah," Kyle said, his green eyes glazed. "But I'll never forget the sight of him falling. I can still hear him screaming."

I walked him to the door after we agreed to save the boat ride for another day. We stood in the doorway, still numb from shock. His hand trembled as it closed over mine. His fingers felt icy. "I was on the stairs just below your house when I saw him fall," he said. "Another minute, and I wouldn't have seen it at all. I would have been at your house, and he would have lain there, until someone wandering along the beach found him."

"If you hadn't seen him fall, *I* might have found him," I said. My stomach heaved at the thought.

"It was ugly. I'm glad you didn't have to see it. His neck twisted like that and his eyes bulging—"

"Kyle, *please*!" The image leapt into my mind, vivid and real.

"I'm sorry," he apologized. "I can't get it out of my head."

"It's okay," I said. "It's just so awful. He was a nice old man."

After I said good-bye to Kyle, I found Mom lying down.

"Another migraine?" I asked sympathetically.

"Afraid so. Stress brings them on sometimes." Her voice was a hoarse whisper. Apparently, Mr. Edwards's accident had gotten to her too. "I'll be okay if I lie down for a while."

I needed to get my mind off Mr. Edwards, so I went to my room and pulled Rita's diary out from where I'd stashed it under my mattress and began reading where I'd left off.

Dear Diary,

Ben and I made up! He said the girl on the beach didn't mean anything to him. So I forgave him. It turns out he was jealous too. He thought I had something going with Shane! Of course, he was wrong. And I'm glad he was jealous. I hope it means he loves me.

I think Ben and I are meant to be together. The only problem is he drinks too much. Once he starts guzzling beer, he drinks till he passes out. And he's grouchy when he's really drunk. I hope he doesn't turn out to be like Mrs. Addison across the street. She drinks like a fish. (Do fish really drink?)

Her son, Greg, joined the army just to get away from her. I told him he'd have to get all his hair cut off and that he'd look dorky in a crew cut, but that didn't stop him. He's actually going to Vietnam!

His mom was yelling at him so much, he probably couldn't think straight. Sometimes she'd yell at him in

*the middle of the night. It woke me up a few times. If
my mom called me names like that I'd die.*

*Of course, my parents do other things I hate. They
made me take that job at the T.S. Factory in Seattle
with those creeps in the white coats. T.S. is in this tall
building about twenty stories high. It sticks up way
above the other Seattle buildings and you can see it
from the Space Needle. Ben and I went up in the
Space Needle one Friday night and I was so dizzy I
got sick to my stomach. That thing is about six hundred feet tall! You can look all over Seattle from the
top.*

Six hundred feet? She thought that was *high*? I
guess the Space Needle must have seemed tall to the
people in the twentieth century. I pictured the Space
Needle as it must have looked a hundred years before.
If it was the tallest structure there, it would have stood
out for miles around. Now it was a quaint relic,
dwarfed by the surrounding buildings. I'd noticed it
when my family had dinner at the top of the 3,000
foot tall Puget Tower across the street from it. As we
ate, I looked down and commented on the strange
shape of the Space Needle.

"There used to be an amusement park called Seattle
Center surrounding the Space Needle," Dad said. "My
great-grandfather attended the World's Fair there in
1962. His mother refused to go up in the Space Needle because she was afraid it would fall over. She didn't
think anything so tall could stay standing for long."

We'd laughed at the irony of it. Now, I found myself thinking of how much things had changed since

Rita's time. There were no floating cities then or cures for cancer. People butchered live animals like cows, pigs, and chickens to eat instead of simulated meat. Cars ran on gasoline instead of solar power. There were no virtual reality computers or underwater homes.

As primitive as Rita's time was, I was strangely drawn to it. What would it have been like to live back then? I eagerly began reading again, anxious to hear more about Rita's life.

Anyway, as I was saying about that witch, Mrs. Addison. I just hope she doesn't start in on Chuck now that Greg's gone. Chuck's only nine, and he's kind of a cute kid. He's got a mop of blond hair and a freckled face. Sometimes when his mom locks him out, he comes into our house when we're not home. (We never lock our door because we don't have a key!) Chuck climbs everything. Mom couldn't believe it when she came home from pottery class yesterday and found him on our roof. He'd climbed up the maple tree just like a little monkey. She thought he'd fall and was going to call the fire department to get him down, but he shinnied down the tree before she could pick up the phone.

She called Mrs. Addison and told her that Chuck could have broken his neck and that she should have a talk with him. But Mrs. Addison said he was a resilient kid and hadn't broken anything yet!

Mom was shocked. Of course, Mom thinks she's the perfect mother. Right now she seems more like a jailer than a mother! I'm still on restrictions. "Indefinitely," she said. Ben is allowed to call but not come over! The only time I can see him is at school.

Mom is a hypocrite just like everyone else in her generation. She has a glass of wine every night, and of course that's fine because SHE does it. But just because I had a few beers that went down wrong— OKAY SO I GOT DRUNK! Just because I got a little drunk, she thinks she can ruin my life.

I miss my nightly walks on the beach, but at least I can see the sunset from my bedroom window. I'm sitting on my window seat and a sweet breeze is ruffling the curtains. The sun just went down and the sky is bright red. The water looks like strawberry pop. It's so beautiful, I want to leap from the window and fly into the sky. I can imagine melting into the sunset and becoming those colors. I wouldn't have to worry about anything anymore. I'd just blend with the sky and exist on the colors of the sunset.

"I know how you feel," I said aloud. I closed the diary and leaned my forehead against the cool glass of the windowpane. The sun was setting and the sky was smeared in red.

It was an evening just like this Rita had written about.

It's funny, but I almost felt she was my friend. I looked forward to reading her diary entries. Though I could have read the whole diary in one sitting, I found myself trying to make it last. I'd read just a page at a time. It was almost like having someone to talk to.

Rita was so familiar. It wasn't because she looked

like me. It was more the way she wrote. It was like she was *talking* to me.

She sat right *here,* I realized. She looked out this window through eyes like mine and watched a sunset like this one.

For a fleeting moment, I felt as if I *was* Rita. Sitting here on *her* window seat with *her* face watching *her* sunset.

I suddenly remembered what Suki had said about reincarnation. Was it possible? Could I be Rita, living her life all over again?

Don't be silly! For all I knew she could still be alive. I did some quick calculating. She'd be 117. A lot of people lived to be that old these days. A century ago, you were considered old if you lived to be ninety. But that was before cancer vaccinations and infallible artificial organs.

Excited, I turned on my computer and accessed the newspaper files at the Banbury Library. If Rita had died in Banbury, I'd find the obituary. If she was still alive, maybe I could look her up. It would be fun to see how her life had turned out.

As I scanned the computer files, I was interrupted by a rap on my bedroom door. It creaked opened, and Suki's pale face peered in at me. "Hi. Your mom said I could come up. I heard about Mr. Edwards. Isn't it awful?"

"Come on in," I sighed. "Kyle saw him fall. He was on his way here."

"Kyle really likes you," she said generously. "I can tell by the way he was sitting so close to you today.

You make a really cute couple." A benign smile lit her face. She didn't look at all jealous.

"Well, we're not really a couple."

"Has he kissed you yet?" she asked, perched on the edge of my bed, eager to lap up the details. She could never have Kyle, but apparently the vicarious thrill was good enough for her.

"You'll be the first to know!" I laughed. "How far back do *The Banbury Times* files go?"

"Forever I guess. What are you looking for?"

"I want to see what happened to Rita Mills."

"The girl with your face! She's got to be dead by now. She'd be like a hundred years old."

"One hundred seventeen," I corrected her and typed in "Mills, Rita," and pushed the search button. Within seconds, the computer had located an article and it filled my computer screen. It was the front page of *The Banbury Times* from 1970. My stomach lurched when I read the headline in tall black letters: LOCAL GIRL'S BOYFRIEND EXECUTED FOR HER MURDER.

Benjamin Grand, 18, was executed Thursday for the murder of his girlfriend, 17-year-old Rita Mills. She was found dead of a head wound at Banbury Point last March.

A jury found Grand guilty of battering Mills, causing her death. Prosecutors maintain he committed the murder in a drunken jealous rage.

A wave of nausea swept through me and I leapt from the chair and bolted to the hallway. I made it to the bathroom just in time to be sick. Afterward I splashed cold water on my face and stared at my reflection in the mirror. My face was gray. *My* face. *Her* face. I could picture that face bruised and lifeless, pressed against the sand.

How could he do that to her? She *loved* him!

Trembling, I went back to my room. Suki had turned off the computer. "I read it," she said quietly. "It's really sad. Maybe you better lie down for a while."

I lay on my bed, and Suki covered me with the puff-square, pulling it up around my chin and patting my arm in a motherly fashion.

"How could he have *killed* her?" I said numbly.

"He was drunk." Her brow furrowed in concern. "Maybe he didn't know what he was doing."

"He *murdered* her!" I spat. "Drunk or not! He murdered her in cold blood."

"It was a long time ago," she said softly.

"I want to be alone now."

"I could make you some hot chocolate," she offered hopefully.

I rolled away from her and buried my head under my pillow.

"It would make you feel better," Suki prodded.

"No!" I said sharply. "I don't want any hot chocolate. I want to be *alone*."

"Well, I guess I'll go then." Her voice was flat.

A moment later, I peeked out from under the pillow. Suki was gone, her feelings bruised again. I suppose I could have been a little more tactful, but my mind was so full of awful things to sort out. Mr. Edwards's accident. Rita's murder.

Two tragedies on the same day!

Of course, Rita had died a century ago. But in my mind it had just happened. I felt I'd lost a friend. A friend and a neighbor.

Mr. Edwards was sweet, even if he was crazy.

Crazy.

Everyone said he was crazy because he rambled on about a murder. I sat up straight, knocking the puff-square from my legs in a flash of realization. He was telling the truth!

A girl *was* murdered on the beach. *Rita!* He was talking about *Rita! He wasn't crazy!*

If Mr. Edwards wasn't crazy, then why did he step off Windy Cliff?

7

WHEN I FINALLY SLEPT, I DREAMED OF HANDS. Angry hands. *Murderous* hands. They shoved Mr. Edwards hard from behind, sending his frail body sailing through the sky. When he crashed against the rocks, the hands brushed against each other as if to dust off any trace of murder.

Like a thick fog, the dream clung to my mind all day long. Vague wisps of a nightmare that refused to evaporate. I felt like I was wading through thick pea soup the rest of the weekend.

"You're sure acting strange," Suki said as we trudged up hill toward the school Monday morning. Banbury High was a mile from my house. Banbury Bay doesn't have moving sidewalks like they do in Salem. When developers proposed installing them, the residents fought it. Tourism is big business in Banbury Bay because it's a historical town. The people here want to keep the whole town looking old-fashioned for the tourists.

Walking to school usually cleared my mind, making it easier to concentrate on the teachers' lectures. But this morning I didn't think it was going to help.

"Mars to Jenna!" Suki shouted. She wore a tasteless bright orange sweater, stretched taut around her thick middle. "What's with you today?"

"I'm just thinking," I mumbled.

"What are you thinking about?"

"Mr. Edwards."

"Yeah. Me too. Poor old man. Poor, crazy old man."

"I'm not so sure he was crazy."

"Why do you say that?" she asked, cocking her head and stumbling to a stop.

"He was right about the murder. He wasn't making it up."

"Oh. You mean Rita. I hadn't thought about that. But he had to be crazy, Jenna. He committed suicide! That's nuts!"

"I don't think he stepped off the cliff on purpose."

"I guess he could have fallen," she conceded. "He couldn't see. He might not have known he was at the edge of the cliff."

"I don't think he fell."

"He didn't fall? He didn't jump? What did he do? Fly?"

"He could have been pushed."

Suki's mouth popped into a startled "O." "Why would anyone want to kill an old man?"

"I don't know. But I keep thinking it might have something to do with Rita's murder. He was always talking about it. Maybe someone wanted to shut him up."

"That's kind of farfetched, don't you think? Rita was murdered a century ago! Why would it matter if he talked about it now?"

I was sorry I'd confided in her. Knowing Suki, she would embarrass me again by telling everyone what I'd said.

Beep! Beep! I nearly leapt from my shoes when the sleek green car pulled up beside us, horn honking. Kyle leaned from the window, grinning mischievously. "Wake up, lady!" he teased. "You looked like you were sleepwalking."

Suddenly I felt the clouds in my mind clear. I smiled back at him, drinking in his handsome face. "I'm wide-awake now." I laughed.

He punched in a command on his steering wheel computer, and the passenger door popped open. I scrambled in beside him. Suki was right behind me, but Kyle roared off before she could get in. Glancing into the rearview mirror, I watched her grow small as we sped away. Soon she was an orange dot in the distance.

"You should have waited for her to get in," I said.

"The exercise will be good for her," Kyle said.

"I feel sorry for her." I sighed. "She's always following me around. She's a nice girl, but she wants to spend every minute with me."

"Pathetic."

"It is. I hate to hurt her feelings."

"What else can you do? She's the type who doesn't get the message unless you hit her over the head."

He's right, I thought. Yet I couldn't shake the prickling guilt.

Kyle turned into a parking space in front of the school. Suddenly, his big warm hand was closing over mine. "You look great today, Jenna," he said huskily. "That sweater matches your eyes."

I shivered inwardly with the compliment. The fuzzy gray sweater fit me snugly, and his emerald eyes swept appreciatively over my curves.

"You're here to study *reading, writing, and arithmetic,*" I joked, feeling flustered.

"I'd rather study *you!*"

I ducked out of the car before he could see me blush. The crisp autumn air cooled my warm cheeks. "Aren't the trees beautiful this time of the year?" I said. Ancient maples with reaching gnarled limbs lined the paved parking lot. A sudden breeze rustled the papery red and orange leaves, sending some swirling down around us.

"I'm not looking at the *trees,*" Kyle said pointedly.

"Would you *stop!*" I said with a nervous giggle.

"You *stop,*" he said, touching my shoulder. He turned me to face him. "You're a pretty girl. You must have guys like me telling you that all the time."

Before I could respond, he tucked his thumb under

my chin and gently tipped my face toward his. His lips were soft and sensuous on mine. The kiss was short and sweet and sent my stomach into a spinning somersault. It left me breathless.

Kyle hooked his arm in mine and we strolled toward the building as leaves blew around our ankles. I noticed several girls watching us enviously. *We're becoming a couple!* I thought excitedly.

He walked me to my homeroom and gave me a quick peck on the cheek before he bounded off to his class. I practically floated to my desk, lost in the memory of his kisses, until I *felt* someone staring at me. I turned to see Suki, glaring at me from the desk across from mine.

"Oh, Suki," I stammered. "I guess you're mad because Kyle didn't give you a ride."

"I guess you two wanted to be *alone,*" she said crisply.

Obviously, she'd seen us in the doorway—seen Kyle kiss my cheek. Had she watched the other kiss too? I'd never seen her mad before. She was always so cheery, going along with whatever I wanted. This was a new side of her.

I regarded her intently and she stared back at me. For the first time, I noticed something odd about her eyes. Her pupils had jagged edges, like chocolate cookies that had been nibbled all the way around.

"You're looking at my eyes," she accused.

"Well, yes. Your pupils are a little unusual."

"Uncle Terry says it's genetic, probably inherited from one of my relatives—though I'll never know who. I guess my strange eyes are one more reason for you to think I'm weird."

"I don't think that," I said, but I knew it sounded like the lie it was.

"We're more alike than you know, Jenna," she said hollowly. She no longer sounded mad. Only sad. "Neither of us fits in. Neither of us belongs here."

I stared at her, confused.

"We've both got it, Jenna."

"Got what?"

"PK," she said. "I knew you had it when that diary popped open by itself."

"Huh?"

"Remember when you found the diary in the attic? You opened it with your mind."

"The lock was rusty and it broke."

"*You* broke it," she said, a knowing smile twitching on her lips.

"Maybe I did," I said slowly. "*You* have PK too? Could you control the dice?"

Suki shrugged. "Sort of. But not like Uncle Terry's star pupil. I'm glad I couldn't control those dice the way you could."

"Suki, you make PK sound like a *disease*! I think it's totally frazzin to have this skill."

She shook her head, her eyes watery in her waif-like face.

It occurred to me she might have some answers for me. After all, she was Grady's niece. She probably knew more than I did about what was going on. "Did you inherit your PK from your parents, Suki?"

"From my mother. She had it, but my father didn't have it."

"What do you mean, *had* it? Doesn't she anymore?"

"She's dead. They're all dead. All of my family is *dead*!"

I gasped, shocked. *So that's why she lives with her uncle!* "I-I didn't know. Was it an accident?"

Suki regarded me blankly. "No. They died of old age."

It was a sarcastic reply. Obviously, she didn't want to talk about how her family had *really* died. It was insensitive of me to ask. I vowed to be nicer to her in the future.

Before I could think of something consoling to say, Peter Froyder, our frizzy-haired homeroom teacher, had called the class to order and begun the computer roll call.

Pressing my thumb to the computer screen built into the corner of my desk, I was automatically entered into the school's central computer. When my parents were in school they typed their names into their desk computers for the attendance count. It was too easy to skip school. Mom once admitted she sometimes covered for her friends, typing their names in when they ditched.

Too bad it wasn't easy to skip anymore. The computer reads our thumbprints and instantly knows whose is whose and who is where!

I drifted through the morning, my mind brimming with everything that had transpired the last three days.

There was absolutely no room for the facts my teachers tried to fit into my brain.

Kyle and I ate lunch together. Or rather, *he* ate. My stomach was too full of butterflies to digest my peanut butter sandwich. It was exciting sitting close to him—though it wasn't the most romantic of settings. We were squeezed together at the end of a crowded cafeteria table with a bunch of loud, disgusting athletes.

"If you're not going to eat that, I will," Kyle said, reaching for my sandwich. He devoured it in three bites. "I've been hungry all weekend. It must be the fall air. I always get hungry when it starts to get cold."

"I'm surprised you ate at all this weekend. I didn't have an appetite after Mr. Edwards's accident," I said.

He gulped down half his milk and wiped his mouth on his sleeve. "I never lose my appetite. That wasn't the first time I saw someone die."

"Really?"

"I was with my grandfather when he died. He was old and sick and he hung on for a long time, slowly wasting away."

"How sad!"

"I got to really know him those last days. On his deathbed, my grandfather told me how he'd made our family what it is."

"Rich?" I said and instantly regretted it when Kyle's eyes clouded.

"The Mettleys are about more than money!" he snapped. "My grandfather worked hard to get where he got. It was a struggle for him. I never realized what he went through before. Things were much more complicated than I thought." He suddenly smiled sheepishly, embarrassed by his outburst.

"Kyle's granddad was the first Mettley million-aire," Mike Willoby said. "Kyle here is still coasting off his grandfather's inventions."

Kyle didn't seem to mind when Mike teased him. "Eat your heart out, buddy," he said and tossed an apple at him.

"Too bad you didn't inherit your grandfather's brains," Mike said. "Maybe you could come up with some inventions of your own."

"What did your grandfather invent?" I asked Kyle.

"Several money-making gadgets," Mike answered for him. "Kyle's grandfather was a famous inventor. Didn't you notice his picture hanging in the lobby of Twin-Star Labs?"

"No, I didn't really get a chance to look around much," I admitted.

"We'll fix that!" Kyle said. "If you're not doing anything after school, I'll take you on a tour."

We met in front of the school after my last class and headed straight for the lab. "Twin-Star Labs has been rebuilt since my grandfather's time," Kyle explained. "It used to be brick. That was before they built with fiberglass. The old building didn't make it through the earthquake in 2064."

"What's it like to own a whole building?" I asked, taking in the towering, cream-colored structure.

"I don't own the whole thing. Just a share my grandfather left me. He developed most of his really successful inventions before he was twenty-two."

Kyle showed me around, and I admired the photos of his grandfather and the spacious labs filled with fascinating inventions.

"Do you know anything about PK?" I asked him.

"Sure. My grandfather is the one who started the PK experiments at Twin-Star."

"Do you know that I have—" I stopped in mid sentence. I wasn't sure I wanted him to know about my supposed PK ability. He might think I was strange.

"Were you going to ask if I knew about your PK skills?"

"You *do* know!"

"I'm a shareholder! I keep up on everything. I know about your abilities, Jenna. I'm impressed."

"Really?"

"Really."

"I'm not sure I can actually move things with my mind. I'm a scientist's daughter and have a hard time believing in PK."

"Remember, *I'm* a scientist's grandson. Telekinetic abilities are real. And you have them." He sounded so sure.

"Everyone around here seems to think that. It's like they know things about me I don't know about myself."

"Don't go paranoid on me," Kyle teased.

"I just wish I could get someone to answer my questions."

"That's easy enough. Let's see if Dr. Grady is in his office."

He was there, seated behind a massive shiny desk,

conversing with his computer. He leapt up when he saw me. "What a surprise! I was going to call you, Jenna."

"Sorry to barge in on you, Dr. Grady," Kyle said. "Jenna has some questions for you."

"Yes, of course," he said, and nodded at the two chairs against the wall.

"You're busy," I said, edging back toward the doorway. Dr. Grady's intensity always made me nervous.

"I'm never too busy for you, Jenna. I've been wanting to talk with you too. I was going to give you time to recover from the weekend."

"Recover?"

"Suki told me about your neighbor. It's a terrible shame! I thought you might need some time to get over it."

"Everyone in the neighborhood is still in shock. We all liked Mr. Edwards. It was awful for Kyle too. He saw him fall."

"So Suki told me," Dr. Grady said, shaking his head. "Terrible, terrible thing."

"He was really old," Kyle said. "At least he didn't die a slow death like my grandfather."

Dr. Grady nodded, his mouth twisted in a grim line as if he was remembering Kyle's grandfather. They must have worked together. I wondered if they'd been friends.

"Well, Jenna," Dr. Grady said, smacking his hands together abruptly. "You had some questions for me?"

"Lots of them. I'm having a hard time believing this PK stuff."

"That's understandable. PK goes against everything you believe in. Our solid world, for instance." He rapped sharply on the wall. "You think the only way to touch things is with your hands? In a sense, your mind has hands and your thoughts are its fingers."

I must have looked as confused as I felt, because he began to speak slowly as if trying to explain something to a small, dense child. "Do you know what brain waves are, Jenna?"

"My thoughts?"

"Actually, brain waves are rhythmic shifts of voltage between areas of the brain which result in the flow of electrical currents."

"Oh."

"Even though you can't see these brain waves, they are there. They are real. Some people have a natural ability to control these waves."

"You think I can do that?"

"You were amazing with the dice," Dr. Grady said, his dark eyes sparkling. "Your scores indicate a success level far higher than statistics could account for. In other words, it is statistically improbable for the dice to consistently land on the numbers you were concentrating on."

"So it wasn't a coincidence?" I asked, not completely convinced.

"A coincidence? Highly improbable. As Kyle mentioned, Twin-Star Labs has been involved in researching psychokinesis for many years. As a young man, Kyle's grandfather began experimenting on a device that can actually amplify PK abilities. Once you become more comfortable with your abilities, we'd like you to utilize this device."

"What kind of a device?"

"It's a visor you wear on your head!" Kyle said. "It makes your brain waves stronger."

"Does it hurt?" I asked.

"Of course not!" Dr. Grady said hurriedly. "You know we wouldn't do anything to harm you." He leaned over to the wall safe and punched in a code on the computer lock. When the door popped open he retrieved something that looked like a pair of plastic earmuffs with glasses hooked to the front.

"That's the visor?"

Dr. Grady nodded, slipping it onto his head so it smashed down his wiry brown hair. "I don't want you to be afraid of this. I wouldn't ask you to do anything I wouldn't do. It's important you feel confident."

"If I wear the visor, my PK will be even stronger?"

"Exactly!" Dr. Grady said, his eyes glittering. "The visor is fueled with a unique substance that Twin-Star Labs has spent decades perfecting. When in an active state, this substance appears as rays of light with an energy all their own. These rays pull the electromagnetic energy from your brain waves. This energy is then recycled through the visor, and in the process strengthened by the rays. The rays—now combined with telekinetic energy—shoot out in the direction you choose to focus them. This whole process sounds complicated, but it takes less than a quarter of a second."

"When can I try it?"

Dr. Grady chuckled. "I like your enthusiasm. Soon. Very soon. First I want you to do a few more PK exercises."

He handed me a sealed cardboard box. "There are a dozen metal paper clips inside this box. Without opening it, try to twist the clips into knots."

"You're kidding!"

"I *never* kid, Jenna. The paper clip experiment has been around since the twentieth century. People with far less ability than you have successfully twisted the paper clips through psychokinesis."

"And some of them made them *disappear*?" I said, thinking of Tarynn's remark about my sister making a paper clip vanish.

"Yes, there was a case where a paper clip seemed to disappear. But I don't believe it really did. Our research indicates that the paper clip was simply moved."

"Moved? You mean to a different place?"

"Not necessarily a different place. More likely, it was transported to another *time* via telekinetic energy."

"Is that possible?"

"We believe so. You see, when you're dealing with telekinetic energy, you're dealing with a force that is very different from the tangible matter that scientists have long been comfortable with. Less open-minded scientists than myself prefer to study matter that they can get a grip on, so to speak—things with melting points and measurements that react predictably with the world around them. I'm getting way ahead of myself. Let me just say that as we've learned more about telekinetic forces, we've also learned it's time to throw out some of the scientific theories we've lived by for so long."

He was rattling on and on, as if to distract me from asking about my sister. I wasn't going to let him get away with it. "These other people with PK that you mentioned?"

"Yes?"

"Some of them were pretty talented," I said, fishing for information. "They were talented like my *sister*!"

Dr. Grady smiled slyly. "Is that a question or a statement?"

"A question. Do I have a sister?"

"Jenna, there are some questions I am not at liberty to answer. It's not that I have a problem with you knowing the facts. It's simply not my place to divulge certain things to you."

His secrecy was annoying. "*Whose* place is it to *divulge* these things?" I snapped, surprising myself with my anger.

Dr. Grady seemed unfazed, and Kyle was staring at his shoes. *Did Kyle know? Did he know about my mysterious sister?*

"I suggest," Dr. Grady said slowly, "that you have a talk with your mother."

8

APPARENTLY MOM WAS THE ONLY PERSON "AT liberty" to tell me the truth. As usual, she was lying down with one of her migraines when I got home. It wasn't very nice of me, but I stomped around slamming doors when I realized she was avoiding me again. *She doesn't have a headache!* I told myself. *She just wants to keep me in the dark!*

Despite my anger, a chill crept over me. Whatever she was hiding must be pretty horrible because everyone acted so strangely whenever I tried to get answers. Why did Mom keep lying to me about my sister? Did something terrible happen? Was my sister dead? Why didn't I remember her?

Suddenly, I wasn't so sure I wanted to know the truth. I decided to let Mom sleep and slipped quietly up the stairs to the sanctuary of my room. But my room no longer seemed like an escape from the awful things in the world. For it was *here* I had learned of Rita's murder. And it was here I would finish her story.

I was afraid to open the diary, afraid to come to the end of her life. I placed the musty diary on the window seat beside me, wondering what secrets it held.

Did she know? Did she have any hint at all of what Ben was going to do to her?

My fingers brushed the withered cover. The red vinyl had cracked and flaked off in places, revealing faded cardboard. *Cardboard.*

Is that what Ben was? A cardboard character as one-dimensional as a paper doll? No depth. No love. Only a smiling face with nothing behind it.

Nothing behind it but a violent, murderous streak!

Suddenly, I *had* to know. I had to know if she had any inkling—if it was really possible to be so deluded by love that you would put your heart in the hands of a killer.

I knew reading Rita's words would no longer be enjoyable. It was painful knowing there were no happy endings for the girl so much like me. But reading her diary was the only way to get the answers to the disturbing questions crowding my mind. Hands shaking, I opened the diary and began reading where I'd left off.

Dear Diary,

Tonight I'm sneaking out of the house to be with Ben. I'm going to stuff pillows under my blanket so it looks like I'm there in case Mom peeks in. Then I'm going to crawl out the window and climb down the tree. Grounded or not, I need to see him. I need his arms around me again! We're meeting on the beach. Diary, I'll fill you in on all the details when I get home.

The rest of the page was blank. Devastatingly blank. "Oh, Rita! Be *careful*!" I whispered. "Don't let him hurt you!"

It was like reading a book where someone has told you the outcome. Yet, as I read Rita's words they sounded so immediate. It was almost as if she were there with me—talking to me.

She was going to be killed. And there was nothing I could do to stop it.

My stomach knotted as I turned the page, fully expecting to see more blank pages. I laughed with relief to see the pages crammed with Rita's familiar flowing handwriting.

Diary, sorry I didn't write more in you yesterday. I was too mad. Would you believe Ben stood me up??? I risked getting grounded for the rest of my life to sneak out to see him and he didn't even show up! I sat on our log for two hours, shivering because I didn't bring my coat. (I thought Ben was going to keep me warm!)

Well, I got madder by the minute. I finally gave up and headed for home. Somebody followed me! It was too dark to see who it was, but someone was definitely there. And it wasn't little Chucky or any of the other neighborhood boys. I heard his footsteps, and when I looked back I got a glimpse of him before he ducked behind a tree! I couldn't tell who it was, but he wasn't a little kid. I had the eeriest feeling that whoever it was wanted to hurt me!

The guy was twisted. Instead of meeting Rita he'd watched her from the shadows and then followed her home. You couldn't get any weirder than that.

Poor Rita! Obliviously in love. Never suspecting that Ben had such a horrible black spot on his soul. Was he so jealous of her that he would spy on her even while she waited for *him*?

I shivered, remembering the footsteps I'd heard on the beach. Was it Ben's ghost, following me as he'd once followed Rita?

Maybe he's mistaken me for her, I thought and instantly chided myself. Like I told Suki, I don't believe in ghosts. My imagination was rushing off with me again.

I could not bear to come to the end of Rita's story. As long as there were pages yet to read, she was still alive. At least, I could *pretend* she was still alive. By not finishing the diary, I could look forward to more conversations with her. Maybe the conversations were one-sided—with her doing all the talking and me doing all the listening. But I *liked* listening to her. And I felt somehow, if the tables were turned, she'd be just as glad to listen to me. She wouldn't babble on and on like Suki does.

I gently closed the diary, tucked it under my mattress, and began concentrating on the box of paper clips.

Bending paper clips with your mind is quite a different thing than controlling moving dice. Though it was fun to give myself credit for affecting the dice, I didn't entirely believe I'd really done anything. Despite what Dr. Grady said, I still thought it could have been a coincidence the dice landed on the numbers I'd concentrated on.

I probably wouldn't have even tried to bend those paper clips if it wasn't for Kyle. I closed my eyes, relishing the memory of his kiss. When he brought me home after the tour of the lab, I'd hoped he'd kiss me again. I was so distracted I almost forgot the box of paper clips. He had reached over and touched my elbow as I climbed from the car. Handing me the box of paper clips, he'd said softly, "I know you can do it, Jenna."

It seemed important to him I help with this experiment. He was obviously proud of his grandfather. It made sense he'd want to see his grandfather's work continued.

I wanted Kyle to be pleased with me, to give him a reason to kiss me again! So I cleared my mind of all thoughts—even Kyle—and set the box on my bedside table and began concentrating.

I imagined my mind had a pair of invisible hands. Hands that could reach from my skull and finger the metal paper clips. I visualized those hands caressing the metal, softening the clips with their warmth. Then I pictured the fingers of my mind gently bending the ends of the paper clips before twisting them into mad, pretzel-like shapes.

I concentrated for half an hour, focusing so hard my

head throbbed. Afterward I lay limp and drained on my bed, staring at the box and wishing I could open it to see if I'd had any effect.

My logical side said such a thing was not possible. "What a waste of time," I muttered aloud. "I should have been doing my homework."

As the words left my mouth, the box suddenly teetered on the edge of my nightstand. All by itself, it fell to the floor.

I spent the rest of the night reading about PK. My computer accessed every book and article ever written on the subject. There was a guy with PK ability in the 1960s who was called a "thoughtagrapher" because he could imprint his thoughts on the film inside a Polaroid camera. When it developed, the images he had pictured appeared on the film.

Another guy fixed broken watches simply by concentrating. And a woman claimed to have actually *transported* herself instantaneously to another city. It was hard to believe, but witnesses swore it really happened.

Scientists documented a case of a ten-year-old Idaho boy in 2040 who could transport his teddy bear at will. The article said he put the bear in his closet, concentrated for a few minutes, and the bear appeared on his grandmother's sofa in New York.

"*The toy's molecules were apparently altered, rearranged, and transported via the child's psychokinetic energy,*" parapsychologist Abraham Sloan said. "*Frankly, we do not yet know how this feat was ac-*

complished—only that it was. I was quite skeptical when asked to participate in studying this youngster, but am now convinced this is no hoax."

Other cases documented people who healed broken bones with a touch, made plants flourish through concentration, and "mentally tripped" Olympic runners as they dashed toward the finish line.

"At first," Abraham Sloan continued, "I did not believe mind over matter was possible. But a fellow scientist pointed out skeptics once felt the same way about electricity. They couldn't see it, so they didn't believe it existed.

"PK is similar to electricity in that they were both unfocused forces before scientists discovered them. Once harnessed, they can make an impact on more solid substances. If we can achieve a better understanding of PK, we will be able to accomplish many things."

Daydreaming of the possibilities, I gazed out my window. Sea gulls sliced through the gray morning sky, their shrieks like tortured souls as they dove for fish.

I picked a bird and concentrated on it. Could I stop it in mid flight—send it gliding in the opposite direction? I focused on it as it dipped and soared and finally landed on the beach, completely uninfluenced by my thoughts.

I was about to give up when something red caught my eye. It was my neighbor, Ruby, in a bright red cap, out for a morning walk. She picked her way up the hill toward our house, her breath wispy tendrils evaporating around her wrinkled face.

"Fall, Ruby!" I whispered, and sent my thoughts out to trip her. She huffed along, unaffected. I visualized my mind as a hand with an unending arm. Sharply focused, I reached out through my window, down the paved road, and wrapped my thoughts around her ankle and yanked her off her feet.

I blinked in shock as Ruby's small shape lay still, the shells she'd collected scattered around her. "Oh, no!" I gasped. "I didn't mean it!"

I bounded from my room on rubbery legs, down our swirling staircase and out the front door. She was sitting up, tears sliding down the creases in her cheeks.

"Ruby!" I cried, dropping to my knees beside her. "Are you okay?"

"It's my ankle," she moaned.

"I'm so sorry! Can you stand?"

"You'll have to help me."

I put my arm around her bony back and hoisted her up. Her tiny, trembling body leaned against mine as I helped her toward her home. "Ruby, I feel awful!" I said.

"It's not your fault, dear."

But it *was*!

I didn't mean to do it! My PK abilities hadn't seemed real to me. I was fooling around, testing my skills. I *never* would hurt someone on purpose.

"I don't know what I could have tripped on," Ruby said.

"Maybe a rock?" I asked hopefully.

"I didn't see one. I guess I just tripped on my third foot!" She laughed raspily. "That's my invisible one that trips me up sometimes."

Good! She was making jokes. I hoped that meant she wasn't seriously hurt. But she winced and gasped, her hazel eyes bright with pain, as we hobbled up her porch steps.

Inside, I covered her with a puff-square as she lay splayed across her couch. "Better call my son," she said.

It was almost time for school by the time he arrived to take her to the doctor's. Suki was strolling by as Ruby's son and I helped her into his car. She stopped and stared, still wearing that awful orange sweater she'd had on the day before. "What happened?" Suki asked, her eyes boring into me—*accusing me!*

"It's nothing serious," Ruby said, attempting a shaky smile. "I think I sprained my ankle. Jenna was watching from her window and raced outside to help. Lucky thing she was there!"

"Lucky thing," Suki mumbled.

This day, Suki did not wait for me. She scurried away without a backward glance. *Did she guess?* Did she know I had made Ruby fall? Or was it just my conscience making me paranoid?

Too distraught to deal with school, I went back to bed. I had not slept all night, and could not sleep now.

My new ability frightened me. If I can hurt someone, I worried, what else am I capable of?

Then it occurred to me that Ruby's fall might not

have had anything to do with me. Old people often take spills. It might be just another coincidence. The thought calmed me.

My eyes settled on the sealed box of paper clips, still on the floor where it had landed after falling from the nightstand. Dr. Grady had said not to open it. But I needed to know. If I opened the box and found the paper clips untouched, I could absolve myself of my guilt over Ruby. And I'd forget this PK stuff once and for all!

I ripped open the box, nearly bending my thumbnail off in my haste. I turned the box upside down and shook out the contents. The paper clips fell tinkling to the floor.

Each one was twisted into a crazy tangle.

9

THERE WAS ABSOLUTELY NO ONE TO TALK TO. MOM was still sleeping. Kyle was at school. Dad was at work—not that I would have talked to him anyway. We never had much to say to each other. It's not that we argue. I kind of wished we would. At least that would be *something*. He and I were like a couple of disinterested acquaintances who happened to live in the same house.

He stayed busy with his work, making only occasional polite conversation with me.

Feeling alone, I picked up Rita's diary.

Dear Diary,

Ben hasn't called. He hasn't been at school. Even Shane doesn't know where he is.

It was a long, boring day. After school I had to stop

*in at the T.S. Factory. As usual, Twin-Star had me
jumping through more hoops.*

I felt like I'd been socked in the belly! *Twin-Star?*
Did Rita mean Twin-Star Labs? Is that what she'd
meant when she'd referred to the T.S. Factory? What
in the world did *she* have to do with them? It was too
much of a coincidence!

*Diary, I haven't written much about this, because
I've filled your pages with my favorite subject—BEN!
But since the rat hasn't given me any new material
lately, I guess I'll catch you up on some of the less interesting parts of my life. Like my work at T.S. I'm really tired of those guys messing with my mind. Today I
faked it. I knew I could control those dice but pretended I couldn't.*

I couldn't believe it. Rita had PK power! And she
was working for the same laboratory as I was. My
stomach churned. I felt dizzy. It was like I'd finally
found the missing piece of the puzzle but didn't know
how it fit. As I continued reading, it became clear. Ex-
cruciatingly clear!

*Mom and Dad have totally bought into the B.S. of
those dudes in the white coats. It figures. They're all
from the same generation. Personally, I don't like
being treated like a laboratory animal. I know I have
a gift, but what business is it of theirs?*

*If Mom and Dad want to "share their talents" then
FINE! But why should I? My parents have been into
this psychic stuff since before it was cool to be into it.
They met at a psychic fair when they were in college.
They were attracted to each other partly because they*

both have telekinetic ability. They married, they mated, and—wouldn't you know it?—their darling daughter has twice the ability of either of them! My brother (the lucky duck) inherited Dad's freckles and Mom's artistic ability, but he didn't get any of the PK genes.

I have the gift, so I'm the guinea pig. The scientists keep talking about the future and what "unique abilities" like mine could mean for all mankind. Why are they so hung up on progress? Why can't they mellow out and sit back and watch the grass grow? Why does it all have to be about BIGGER and BETTER?

If you ask me, they're all a bunch of greedy pigs who will never be satisfied with what they have. I want to tell them to "Look around! Dig what's going on!" Of course, they'd never understand.

I think the thing that gets me the most P.O.'d is that they take life so lightly. My parents think it's really cool that a part of them will live after they're dead and gone and "contribute to society." But I think what they did was totally uncool. It just doesn't seem natural!

Let me back up a little, Diary. I get so wound up about this I don't tell it in order. The scientists have some major invention or something that is supposed to come together in the future. They need someone with abilities like mine to help them with it. But I could grow old and die before they get the kinks worked out of the thing. So they asked my parents to put a kid in the freezer! In a cold, clinical laboratory they implanted my mother's egg with my father's seed

*and made an embryo. A test-tube baby! Then they
froze it, to be thawed out at a later date and implanted
in some stranger. Can you imagine? My brother or
sister could be born after I'm dead!*

The diary slipped from my lap and plopped to the
floor. I sat paralyzed, too stunned to pick it up. My
head felt like it was stuffed with cotton, and my
thoughts tumbled clumsily over each other as I tried
to make sense of what I'd just read.

It cannot be possible! But I knew it was true. Rita
was my sister. And I had come from an embryo that
was frozen a century ago.

"Wake up, Mom!" I cried. I yanked the pillow off her
head, and she peered up at me, blinking in the sudden
light.

"What's the matter?" she mumbled. "Are you
sick?"

"We need to talk."

She glanced at the clock. "Jenna, you're late for
school!"

"I'm *late* for a lot of things!" I spat. "About a hundred years late!"

"What are you talking about?" Her voice came out
strangled, and her face was as pale as a summer moon
at dusk.

"You *know* what I'm talking about. Please stop
lying to me!"

"Okay," she said simply. "Get me a cup of coffee
and let me gather my thoughts."

"No more lies?"

"I was only trying to protect you!"

"Mom! The *truth*?"

She nodded and swung her thick bare legs from the bed and nervously smoothed down her cotton nightgown. I rushed to make coffee, and we were soon huddled in the breakfast nook.

Mom's stubby fingers wrapped around her coffee cup and she stared into the muddy liquid, avoiding my gaze. "Who told you, honey?"

"I found an old diary in the attic. It belonged to Rita Mills. She wrote about the frozen embryo, and I knew it was me."

"Dear God!"

"I know now Rita was my sister. My *real* mother put me on ice a century ago."

"I'm your real mother! I did everything a mother does. I carried you for nine months. I had morning sickness, swollen ankles, stretch marks. I was in labor with you for twelve hours—"

"Can we skip the speech!" I cut her off nastily. She winced, and I knew I had hurt her. But I didn't care.

"Okay, Jenna," she said slowly. "I admit I am not your biological mother. But I love you more than my own life. I understand you're hurt and confused. For seventeen years I've dreaded this conversation. I tried to put it off as long as possible."

"You lied to me. My whole life is a lie! I don't even know who I am!"

"You are Jenna Jean Jacobsen, my *daughter*. You are a beautiful, talented girl."

"I'm a freak."

"Don't say that, Jenna."

"Just tell me how this happened!"

"Over a century ago, in the 1950s, Bonnie Booth, a relative of an ancestor of mine, married Steven Mills," she began. "This couple both had an extraordinary talent that was of great interest to scientists."

"Yes, I know! They had PK abilities. They were Rita's parents, right?" I said. "Do you mean to tell me that Rita's mom was an *ancestor* of yours?"

"Yes. She was my great-great-grandmother's sister."

"So you and I are related?"

Mom's dewy eyes sought mine. "I'm your *mother*! Of course, we're related."

"Yeah, yeah, yeah," I muttered. "What am I to you? A distant cousin?"

"Jenna, *please*!"

"Go on then," I said, barely containing my outrage. "Finish the story."

"In the early 1950s, several Twin-Star Lab scientists secretly explored the idea of freezing embryos— though it wasn't until years later that the procedure was independently discovered and publicized by another group. The Twin-Star scientists knew that when Steve's and Bonnie's genes were combined, there was a high likelihood they would produce a child with PK ability stronger than both of them put together. Of course, it wasn't a sure thing. You never can tell what you're going to get when you have children. It's kind of a grab bag of genes. Sometimes kids get their parents' brains or musical talent and sometimes they inherit their great-uncle Harry's temper. Bonnie and Steve's daughter, Rita—"

"*My sister!*"

"Yes. Your biological sister seemed to have inherited the ability. But they didn't know this at the time they froze the embryo. Rita was still an infant, and they were struggling financially. They didn't think they could afford to raise more children. But a few years later they had a son. He showed no sign of psychic ability at all."

"How did they know *I'd* have the ability?"

"No one really knew. They hoped you would. Another woman with PK ability also donated an embryo. The scientists hoped one of the embryos would have the talent they were looking for."

"How can someone *donate* their child to science?" I asked, as salty tears stung my eyes.

"I don't know, honey, but I'm sure they never meant to hurt you."

"How did I end up with you?"

"Bonnie Mills wanted to make sure you had a family member looking after you. She had papers drawn up that said when and if the embryo was implanted, a descendant of her family would be appointed as guardian. I inherited the guardianship to the embryo. No one could touch the embryo without my approval. Actually, I didn't know you existed until I met your father."

"You mean your *husband*! He's never been a father to me."

"He tries. He's not sentimental. His brain doesn't

work that way. But I know he cares for you in his own way. Your dad was working for Twin-Star and they were progressing on a top secret experiment. They were ready to implant the embryo but needed me to sign a release."

"That's how you met Dad?" I asked, incredulous.

A faint smile touched her lips. "He came to my apartment with the documents. He wasn't exactly handsome, but there was something about him. We ended up going out for dinner."

"That's when you signed the papers?"

"No, I wouldn't do it. They wanted to implant you in a surrogate mother who had no interest in raising you. They ended up doing that with the other baby. That child was raised by scientists in a clinical environment. She's a complete misfit. Your father and I fell in love. I wanted a child desperately! My first marriage ended in divorce after I was unable to conceive a child. I'd actually considered in vitro fertilization during my first marriage. But Roy and I split up."

"Roy?" I squeaked. "Why didn't you tell me you were married before?"

"I was afraid it would lead to more questions," she said quietly. "Jenna, I was afraid for you to learn about the things I'm telling you. I didn't know how you'd react."

My head throbbed. It was as if I was suddenly viewing my world through an old time fun house mirror. Everything was twisted and distorted and completely unreal. "So when did you decide to have me?" I asked.

"As soon as your dad and I got engaged. It seemed like the right thing to do. I wanted a baby, and you needed to be born. I worried, though, because I knew if you developed PK abilities I'd have to allow you to help Twin-Star with their experiments. Bonnie Mills had signed the contract agreeing to that stipulation. Of course I didn't like it. Living with your father, I've seen how overzealous scientists can get. I worried they'd get you involved in something dangerous. I secretly hoped you wouldn't inherit any PK skills."

"What right did she have to make decisions for me?"

"Who?"

"My real mother!" I screamed, as a hot wave of hysteria shot through me. "How *could* she?"

"Honey, please," Mom pleaded as I leapt up from the table. "I know this is upsetting. Take a deep breath and listen to me."

"Why should I?"

"This is exactly what I was afraid of! See, this is why I kept this a secret. I knew you'd be upset."

"If you knew, then why did you do it?" I yelled at her. "Why did you let me be born a hundred years after my time?"

"The alternative," she said slowly, "was to let you never be born at all."

10

I FOUND THE FAMILY PICTURES IN OUR COMPUTER files. All I had to do was trace Mom's family tree back a few generations and there they were. Bonnie. Steven. Rita. Jim.

My family.

They stared at me from my computer screen, frozen in the typical poses of their era. Bonnie and Steve at their wedding, arms entwined as they fed each other bites of white cake. She had my gray eyes and button nose. He had my thin lips and lopsided smile.

After the wedding pictures came the baby photos. Even in the blurry old photographs, the adoration showed on their faces as they took turns holding the baby in the dozens and dozens of photographs. They loved her as they would never love me.

They didn't even give me a chance to know them!

Rita's toddler and kindergarten pictures were followed by photos of my brother Jim. He was a mischievous-looking little boy with fire-red hair in looping curls. Rita had written in her diary that he was a brat who drove her crazy. I'd have given anything to have been there with her, having our little brother drive us crazy together.

In a matter of moments I watched Rita's life unfold as the computer scrolled through the photos. She was a gap-toothed kindergartner smiling cheerfully at the camera, then a gangly nine-year-old hanging upside down in a tree. In the seventh grade her hair was styled in a puffy bouffant as she posed primly. But as she traveled into her teen years, her hair flowed unrestrained down her shoulders, sometimes falling messily into her sullen eyes.

I could see now we weren't identical. All the photos with so many different angles revealed new sides to Rita. Her forehead was higher than mine, her eyes a little wider spaced. I had a widow's peak, while her hairline was flat. My chin was slightly sharper, and my mouth rose higher on the left when I smiled. But the differences were subtle, and the resemblance was still strong. We looked as much alike as you could expect two sisters to look.

The family portraits made me saddest. The last one of all four of them together was a formally posed portrait against a studio backdrop of a sunny ocean scene. Seventeen-year-old Rita sat beside Jim. Our parents stood behind them, arms around each other. Jim's face was chubby and his curls were cropped short. The photographer must have told a good joke, because everyone was grinning broadly.

I should have been there, filling the empty space between my brother and sister—laughing with them! I squinted at the photo, imagining myself in the space between them.

How could they have lived their whole lives without me?

Renewed anger bubbled up inside me.

My family—my history—had passed by without me. *How could they have let that happen?* I wanted to shout at them the way I had shouted at Mom. But they were dead. And it's not very satisfying to yell at dead people.

Part of me felt guilty for being mad at them. After all, they were gone and couldn't defend themselves. But then I got even angrier at them for making me feel this way. I hadn't *asked* for this! They had put me in this situation with no thought for my feelings.

I scrolled to the next photograph. It was another family portrait, this time minus Rita. Jim had outgrown his chubbiness. He was now tall and gawky, his chin squared off.

Nobody smiled in this picture. Our mother had shadowy smudges beneath her eyes and our father's hair was touched with white.

The date under the photograph indicated it had been taken a year after Rita's murder.

"Oh, Rita," I said aloud. "If only I'd been there with you. I wouldn't have let him hurt you."

What had become of the rest of them? My hands

were trembling too much to type in the command for the obituaries. I flicked the computer switch to voice command mode. "Computer," I said. "Find the obituary for Bonnie Mills. I don't know the year of her birth. She probably died in Seattle."

An instant later I was reading about my real mother's death. At eighty-five her body gave in to bone cancer after she'd spent a lifetime active in a long list of clubs and organizations.

My father died in a plane crash at age fifty-eight. The violence of it made me shudder. The man with my smile smashed against a mountainside in a small private plane and perished in the flames.

Dull with shock, I asked the computer about my brother. "Computer, find an obituary for James Peter Terrance Mills, born in Seattle, Washington, in 1959."

"Scanning, scanning, scanning," the computer replied in its canned ladylike voice.

"Search negative," it finally said. "No obituary for James Peter Terrance Mills."

"Maybe I have his birth year wrong. Computer, check the obituaries for any James Peter Terrance Mills born between 1955 and 1965. Do a nationwide search."

"Scanning, scanning, scanning. Search negative."

Was it possible? I wondered, excitement rising within me. *Could he still be alive?*

It was simply too much to hope for. Yet, it was not impossible. If he was still alive, my baby brother would be 111 years old!

"Computer," I commanded, "scan *The Banbury Times* for any articles on James Peter Mills."

My screen was soon filled with an article from 2020, about teacher of the year James Peter Mills. A plump, red-haired man sat atop a big square desk, surrounded by fifth grade students.

"Mr. Mills makes math fun!" says fifth grader Eric Moore about his all-time favorite teacher, the article began. *Judging by the enthusiasm of his students, it's no wonder James Mills, 60, won the "Teacher of the Year" award.*

I scanned the rest of the story. It was sweet, but unrevealing. Apparently, my brother had dedicated his life to teaching. He hadn't even married. At least not at that point. Who knew what he'd done in the last forty years?

"I think you should stop worrying about it," Kyle advised me as we strolled along the beach.

He had popped in unexpectedly after school, and I hadn't been able to hide the fact I'd been crying. My red eyes gave me away.

It was a sunless, silver afternoon with fat clouds threatening rain. A brisk breeze skimmed over the gray waves, sending an occasional spray of icy water toward us.

As we walked and talked, Kyle admitted he knew everything. "I wanted to tell you, but I was ethically bound to keep the secret."

"*Ethically?* I can't think of anything more unethical than what's been done to me."

"Look at it this way," he said, sliding his hand along my back. "If you'd been born last century, we never would have met."

I smiled in spite of myself as he pulled me against him. His tangy after-shave filled my nostrils. He always smelled so good.

"You'd be dead now, Jenna," he whispered against my neck. "Your life would already be over. Did you think about that?"

I pressed my cheek against him as his strong arms enveloped me. His chest was rock solid, and his sweater so soft as his heartbeat danced in my ears.

"I'm glad you're here now, Jenna."

"You don't think I'm a freak?"

"I think you're beautiful."

"But I'm a hundred years older than you," I pointed out.

Laughing, he said, "I always wanted to date an older woman."

It was so ludicrous I laughed too. My laughter seemed to carry away the tension. It evaporated on the breeze with my giggles.

"I'm glad to hear you laughing," Kyle said. "You have to put the past behind you. That's the healthiest thing to do."

Hand in hand, we traveled south along the curved beach, and ended up sitting atop what looked like a giant, jagged black rock. Thousands of barnacles clung to its base, and its side were slick with seaweed.

Kyle found a foothold and climbed up first. I was amazed at his strength as he pulled me up beside him.

The rock was fifteen feet tall and the top was dry with a hollowed-out area, perfect for sitting. "What a strange-looking rock," I said, settling in beside him.

"Actually, it's a cave," he explained, as we peered through a crack at the foamy water below. "There's a tide pool inside. When I was a kid we'd come down here and catch hermit crabs for pets. There's a small hole in the side of the cave we crawled through."

"This must be Crab Cave," I said with a gasp. "My dad said they found a skeleton in here twenty years ago."

"I heard about that. I wonder who it was."

We sat silently watching the tide slither in. Waves crept in and out of the cave—each one rushing in as if terribly curious about the dark secrets the cave held, only to retreat slowly, shocked and disturbed by what it had learned.

The skeleton was gone, but I could not stop thinking of it. In a sense, we were sitting on a man's grave. The thought made me shiver.

"Are you cold?" Kyle asked, slipping his arm around me.

"I'm okay."

"*Are* you?" His pupils had grown large, nearly filling his soft green eyes. He looked so concerned, it made me smile. "I like your smile," he said. "I hope you're not going to be upset anymore."

"I've got a lot to sort out. The things I found out today are so hard to believe."

"You should put it all behind you."

"I can't do that. My brother might still be alive. I want to meet him."

"Why?"

"He's my *brother,*" I said. "He's *family!*"

"All you share are common genes. You haven't had any of the same experiences. It's not as if you could reminisce."

How could he understand? His family tree had sprouted in the natural order. His ancestors came before him, his descendants would come after him. He had a place in the middle of a big happy family. Everything in Kyle's life was lined up as it should be.

How do you explain what it feels like to be yanked from the natural orders of things? I was the first cousin of my own mother's *ancestor*! Some of my relatives' descendants had already grown old and died. My family was dead. And despite Kyle's strong arms around me, I felt terribly, terribly alone.

"No one can understand how I feel," I said.

As it turned out, I was wrong. I spent the next morning with the one person who knew exactly how I felt.

11

EARLY WEDNESDAY MORNING, I DRESSED HURRIEDLY and left the house. I did not want to see or talk to my mother—or rather, the woman I'd *thought* was my mother!

I'd never forgive her! She had betrayed me by lying to me my entire life. It didn't matter that she had justified the lie by claiming she was trying to protect me. I could not forget the fact she had repeatedly lied to me about who I was.

I didn't want to be home, and I didn't want to be in school. Instead, I took the solar-bus to the mall where I plopped down on a bench on the moving sidewalk. There I sat, watching the stores drift past as the sidewalk moved along its never ending path around the circular mall.

The pungent aroma of brewing coffee mingled with

the fresh, clean scent of new clothes. Shoppers bustled about, their canvas bags bulging with purchases as they hopped on and off the sidewalk. Canned voices emanated from the shops, announcing sales and specialty items. I closed my eyes, losing myself in the reassuring sounds and smells of the mall.

Suddenly, a familiar male voice pricked my ear. "I've never felt like this about anyone before," he said. My eyes flew open. *That sounds like Kyle!* I sat upright, straining to hear.

"I feel the same way about you, Kyle," a soft, feminine voice replied. She too sounded familiar. "Let's order some champagne to celebrate our engagement."

I stepped off the sidewalk and slipped through an arched doorway toward the sound of the conversation. I found myself in a long dark hallway, with dozens of doors on each side. Apparently, I'd stumbled onto a new restaurant with private dining rooms.

Delicious, buttery aromas drifted through the slightly open door of the closest room. "Let's make a toast, sweetheart," Kyle said. He was apparently having a romantic breakfast with his girlfriend. My stomach churned with jealousy as I turned away, ready to step back onto the sidewalk when he said, "You are the most beautiful girl I've ever seen, Suki."

Suki? Something very strange was going on. I moved toward the doorway and peered in. There was Kyle, his eyes filled with love as he gazed at Suki across a linen tablecloth decorated with silver candlesticks.

I gasped involuntarily. Suki turned her head

sharply. "Jenna!" she cried, sounding very embarrassed.

"I'm sorry!" I mumbled, turning to go.

"Don't leave, Jenna," she said. "You've already seen. You might as well stay."

"Suki, darling, I long to hold you in my arms," Kyle said as if he hadn't even noticed my intrusion.

"Computer, end program." Suki said. Kyle and the beautiful table instantly disintegrated as bright lights filled the room. Suki sat by herself in a nearly empty cubicle.

"Oh!" I cried. "This is the new virtual reality arcade you were telling me about! I thought Kyle was really here!"

"I *wish*," Suki said. "He seemed really real, didn't he?"

"Everything did. I even smelled the omelet."

"I programmed that in. You can write your own program and make people do whatever you want them to."

"How did you make Kyle seem so real?"

"I got ahold of a videotape of him, put it in the computer, and it did the rest. But you can get the same effect with photographs. All I've got left of my mother is three still photographs. I fed those into the computer and came up with a program where she talks to me and apologizes for what she did. It makes me feel a little better."

"Apologizes? What did she do to you?"

"The same thing your real mother did to *you*, Jenna."

My mouth fell open, and I stared at her as if seeing her for the first time.

"My mother sold me to science so she could buy a new car," Suki said.

"*You* were the other embryo?"

"I tried to tell you before. Of course, Uncle Terry would have had my head if I had. He promised your mother no one would tell you the truth. She called Uncle Terry yesterday, really upset because you'd found out. She tried to get him to let you off the hook with the experiments." She added wistfully, "I wish I had someone like that to care about me."

"You have your uncle Terry."

"Obviously, he's not really my uncle. All my family died decades before I was even born. Dr. Grady makes me call him Uncle Terry because he thinks it will make me *feel* like I have a family. But he doesn't really care about me. Especially since my PK ability hasn't lived up to his expectations."

"So *you* were the baby who was raised by the scientists," I said. "My mom said there was another frozen embryo. But I didn't realize it was *you*."

"I told you we're alike!"

"I guess we do have something in common," I admitted.

"Do you want to try the virtual reality computer? You could program in your real family and have a conversation with them."

The idea was appealing. My computer at home had a modem, so I was able to access all the family pictures without leaving the VR arcade simply by typing in our computer's confidential code. The virtual reality computer recorded all the different angles of my family's faces and fitted them on bodies in its own computer files.

I had no idea what my family sounded like, so I used my voice as a guideline. The computer slightly distorted my voice to create voices for my mother and sister. I let the random selector pick voices for my dad and brother.

Then I selected a previously written "happy family gathering" program, and set it in a park.

After asking Suki to wait for me outside, I shut the door and said, "Computer, begin program."

Lush green trees sprang up around me as a fragrant summer breeze filled the air. Birds chirped and golden sun rays fell upon the clearing where I stood.

"Jenna, where are you?" a soft voice called. An instant later, my mother—my *real* mother—stepped through the trees, a wicker picnic basket dangling from her arm. She smiled at me. It was the same face from the frozen photographs, but now it was animated. *Alive!*

Her eyes twinkled and blinked, her chest rose and fell with her breaths, and a strand of soft brown hair blew across her face with the breeze.

"Mother?" I whispered.

"You found a great spot for our picnic," she said and cupped her hands around her mouth. "Steven! Rita! Jim! Come see the wonderful spot that Jenna has found for us."

The rest of my family burst upon the scene, laughing happily.

"Rita!" I cried at the sight of my sister.

"What, Jenna?" she asked as she knelt beside the picnic basket, spreading out a checkered tablecloth. I studied her profile as she turned her head and pointed up at the tree. "Did you see the squirrel, Jenna? Maybe he'd like some potato chips."

"It's like you're really here," I said in awe. "It's so real."

She grinned at me as the breeze lifted her long hair off her neck.

"But you're *not* real, are you?" I asked.

"Of course we are," Rita said.

"No! You're dead. You can't be real."

"Don't be silly," she replied, but I knew it was only the computer, talking for her.

"How could you have lived your whole life without knowing me?" I asked, as tears warmed my eyes. The three figures stared at me, still grinning.

"Wipe those stupid smiles off your faces!" I cried. "Answer my question!"

"How about a piece of pie?" my mother asked, slicing into a plump apple pie.

"Answer my question! Why did you die without knowing me?" I demanded, my voice rising in fury. The figures around me froze. The breeze abruptly ceased and the sun faded.

"Anger inappropriate for this program," a high-pitched computer voice interrupted. "Would you like to select another mode?"

"No," I said. "Forget it. End the program!" The golden-green scene vanished, taking my family with it. I stared at the stark cubicle around me, feeling more alone than ever. Trying to re-create my family had been a stupid idea. It was pathetic. As pathetic as Suki and her virtual reality fantasy about Kyle.

"It's better if you write your own program," Suki informed me when I met her outside. "If you pick one from the computer files, it's never personal enough to seem real."

"It wouldn't matter if I spent a thousand hours writing a program," I said.

"I could help you with it," she said, her voice shrill with excitement. "We could make it so realistic you wouldn't believe it."

"Don't you get it, Suki? It wouldn't matter! It wouldn't matter because no matter how real it *seemed,* it wouldn't *be* real."

"Maybe not," she said sadly. "But it's all we have."

That might be true for her, I thought. But I still had someone left. "My brother is alive," I said. "And I'm going to find him."

Suki and I parted at noon. She headed down the beach as I unlocked our front door. I was relieved to find that Mom had gone out. I knew I couldn't avoid her forever, but I wasn't ready to talk to her yet.

My virtual reality experience had left me strangely empty. The phony computer family may have looked real, but their lack of soul had only served to mock me, reminding me of what I could never have.

I cracked open Rita's diary. *Now* she was with me. I lovingly brushed my fingers over the slanted, looping words she had created with a purple pen. The Rita who leapt to my mind as I read was more real than any virtual reality program could ever create.

Dear Diary,

I've yet to hear from Ben! Shane said Ben got a fake I.D. and is out hitting all the bars instead of going to school. It sounds like I've fallen in love with a certified alcoholic. Diary, I have to admit that I'm scared for him. He's obviously not taking care of himself, and that frightens me. What if something awful happens to him while he's drunk?

There is something else that's scaring me. I've had this really eerie sensation that SOMEONE has been following me. I was almost sure someone was in the bushes last night, staring up at my window. I told my parents, but they just laughed. They said I've been watching too many horror movies.

You'd think that my parents, of all people, would trust my psychic instincts. Well, I guess they don't have much faith in me since I've proved a dud in the PK department. As I mentioned earlier, I faked it with those scientists. I pretended I didn't have any PK ability at all. Dr. Crowell and his CUTE assistant (who I would like to date if I wasn't in love with Ben) are the only ones who know I really do have PK talent. That's because I've been helping them on a secret project. They're so excited about it that I couldn't let them down.

As for the rest of those boring dudes in white, I let

them think I'd lost all my psychic ability. I guess it's backfiring on me, because now my own parents won't believe me that I SENSE something awful is about to happen.

I wish someone would listen to me. I wish someone would believe me! Something evil is in the air. It's all around us, closing in, and I don't know what to do.

It was as if Rita was speaking directly to me. Though her words were written long ago, the years had not silenced them. Her thoughts were there before me, in a lavender ink that had softened over the decades into a pale, whispering shade. Her words were no longer the bright, purple shouts that must have spilled so dramatically from her pen a century ago.

Time had faded the flowing words, but it had not completely hushed them. They were like whispers— desperate whispers urging me to listen to her. They were whispers from the grave.

"I believe you, Rita," I said aloud. "And I would have done *anything* to keep you safe. If only I'd been there."

My sister knew she was in danger. Yet, she did not guess the boy she loved would be the one to kill her. I gently closed the diary. Perhaps there would be another page for me to read tomorrow. Perhaps not.

As I sat grieving for my sister, soft thudding footsteps sounded on the stairs outside my room. *That's strange,* I thought. *I didn't hear Mom's car pull up.* "Mom, is that you?" I called out.

An eerie silence followed. "Mom?" I crossed the

room, opened my bedroom door, and peered into the dark hallway. Footsteps, fast and furious, thumped down the steps. Somebody was in our house!

My stomach dove to my knees as I slammed my bedroom door. With shaky hands, I slid the lock into place. Would the flimsy little lock keep out an intruder?

Our front door slammed. *They've left,* I thought, sagging against the door with relief. But then something occurred to me. How did I know they'd left? It could be a trick. Whoever it was could be downstairs waiting for me.

12

THE STEADY KNOCK OF MY HEARTBEAT ECHOED IN my ears as I held my breath and listened. The idea of staying in the house filled me with stomach-twisting terror. But there was no way I was going down those stairs!

I chose the route that Rita sometimes took. I opened my window and climbed into the outreached arms of the maple tree. Leaves, wet and fragrant, tickled my face as I shinnied down the trunk.

When my toes brushed the earth, I bolted away from the house, fearful that the intruder might emerge and grab me.

Someone called my name, and I turned to see Ruby hobbling out onto her porch with a walker. "I saw someone running out of your house a few minutes ago," she said.

"Who was it?" I cried.

"I didn't get a good look at him. I saw him from the back as he was running away. Actually I can't say for sure if it was a man or woman."

"Which way did he go?"

"Toward the beach, I think."

"I was upstairs when I heard someone on our stairs. Our front door slammed, but I wasn't sure if he left. I'm glad you told me."

"Well, that's what neighbors are for. We look out for each other. You were a big help to me when I fell."

"How is your ankle?" I asked, swallowing the guilty lump in my throat. "Should you be walking?"

"I'm not putting any pressure on it. It's been better, but it will mend. You should call the police and tell them about your burglar."

"Okay. First I'll look around and see if anything's missing."

Relieved to learn the intruder had left, I went back inside. Everything seemed just as it should be. If it had been a burglar, I must have scared him away before he could steal anything.

I didn't call the police. I wasn't up for explaining to the officers why I wasn't in school.

Nervous now about being home alone, I decided to leave and try to track down my brother. On a whim, I asked our computer to access the phone directory. To my amazement, my little brother was listed there. He was living on Deep Brine Island, a retirement home on a man-made island that floats in Puget Sound, several miles off the shore of Seattle.

Route XYZ on the solar-bus heads straight for Deep Brine Island. It travels three hundred miles an hour on a thin silver track, and since my destination was twenty miles away, I could expect to be there in four minutes.

The back of my neck prickled as I boarded the bus, as if unwelcome eyes were examining me. I turned quickly, scanning the station crowd, but an impatient lady behind me nudged me up the bus stairs. I found a seat, telling myself I was jumpy because of the burglar.

All thoughts of the intruder vanished as the solar-bus soared over Puget Sound on a sparkling track that rises fifty feet above the waves before sloping gently to Deep Brine Island. All I could think of was my brother when I spotted the island crammed with tall pink buildings. He was actually *there*—perhaps sitting in one of the thousands of windows that winked in the sunlight.

He would no longer be the mischievous red-haired youth I'd come to know from my family photos. He might not even resemble the middle-aged teacher of the year from the old article.

Shivering with anticipation, I found his building and knocked on his apartment door—only to be disappointed when no one answered. Where was he? Had I waited too long to find him? Had he *died*?

Drawing deep calming breaths, I headed for the nearby cluster of shops along the water's edge. I would pass some time looking for a gift for Ruby, and then return to my brother's apartment and wait for him.

The island swarmed with white-haired, wrinkled people. Most were robust and healthy-looking as they strolled along the sidewalks. Cars were nonexistent here, but a few solar-powered wheelchairs zipped along the roadways.

I bought strawberry jam and imported English biscuits for Ruby, and then got myself a cup of hot chocolate. As I sat sipping it, I smiled at the old folks who ambled in and out of the shop.

An old guy passing my table stopped suddenly as his eyes met mine. His knees seemed to buckle beneath him, and I leapt up and grabbed his arm. Had I done it again? Had I unconsciously made an old person fall?

"Rita?" he asked raspily.

The familiar name he spoke told me who he was. For a long moment, all I could do was stare. The same gentle blue eyes of the old photos peered out from the creased face. The man's hair was coarse and gray, but his eyebrows were fire-red. An overwhelming wave of love surged in me. I reached across the smooth tabletop and squeezed his withered hand. "Sit down," I said. "I'm not Rita, but I *am* a relative. I've been looking for you."

My brother sat across from me, breathing raggedly. "I thought I'd seen a ghost," he admitted, smiling with embarrassment. "I thought maybe it was time to meet my maker. You're the spitting image of my sister. I figured she'd finally come for me. You say you're a relative?"

"This might come as a shock. Did you know that your parents gave a frozen embryo to science?"

"Good Lord!" he cried hoarsely. "Are you telling me that's *you*?"

"Yes, Jim. I'm your sister."

His shaky hand reached out and stroked my hair. "I tried to find out about you over thirty years ago," he said softly. "They told me they didn't know if you'd be born in my lifetime. I wasn't a candidate for your guardianship because of the way the wills were written."

"My mom is a descendant from your family," I explained. "She was my legal guardian and I was implanted in her. She's Ashley Fraser's niece."

"I remember Ashley. She inherited the family's home. Ashley was my cousin's niece. Real nice gal. I lost touch with her years ago."

"She died last summer. I live in your house now."

"Well, I'll be," he said. "It's like the closing of a circle. You helped pay for that house. It's only right you live there now."

"What do you mean?"

"The money our parents got for you paid for the down payment."

"Our parents *sold* me?" Shocked tears rolled down my face.

"Now, honey, please don't be upset. I thought you knew."

"How *could* they?"

"Oh, me and my big mouth! They didn't do it for the money. They wanted the future to be brighter for everyone—including *you*. But I think Mom regretted her decision later."

"Really?" I asked, blowing my nose on a napkin.

"Yes. She worried about what your life would be like. But our parents were young when they got involved with Twin-Star, and thought they were doing a good thing when they agreed to freeze an embryo. They hoped the work at Twin-Star would make the whole world a better place."

"I know Rita didn't like what they did!"

"How do you know that?"

"See this?" I said, slipping the diary from my jacket pocket. "I found it in our attic. That's how I found out about all of you. I thought you might like to see it."

"Rita's diary," he said fondly and fingered the cover. "I'm glad you have this. All my family mementos were destroyed in a fire."

"I can send you copies of some family photographs," I offered. " "Our computer is full of them."

"I'd appreciate that. This diary brings back memories. I used to sneak into her room and read it. She'd have killed me if she'd known."

"Mostly she wrote about her boyfriend."

"*Ben!*" He jerked his fingers away, as if the diary had given him an electrical shock. "If the state hadn't given him the death sentence, I would have killed him myself."

"I hate him too," I admitted.

"Oh, he was smooth," Jim said through gritted

teeth. "And he had my sister wrapped around his little finger. She thought he was so charming, but I didn't like the way he drank. He destroyed our family when he killed her."

"It must have been horrible."

"Worse than that. And the trial dragged on for months. Those idiot defense attorneys tried every trick in the book to get that killer off the hook. First they dragged in an unreliable witness and put him on the stand—a neighbor boy who was a known liar and couldn't possibly have seen the killing. They coached him into saying Ben didn't do it. When that approach didn't work, the attorneys blamed it on the alcohol. They said Ben was so drunk he didn't even *remember* it. They said the alcohol clouded his judgment and he shouldn't have to be responsible for the murder. The jury didn't buy it."

"Good. If he'd gotten off the hook, he might have done it again."

"Ben sobbed on the stand—said he never meant to hurt Rita," Jim said bitterly. "But I knew he was crying for himself. My family was never the same afterward. The trial was particularly hard on Mother."

The talk of Rita's murder was wearing on him. His sagging skin was slightly gray, and his words rolled out slowly.

Promising to stay in touch, we hugged and said good-bye.

Home fifteen minutes later, I went straight to my room without greeting my mother.

As awful as it was, I wanted to read more about

Rita's murder. *If I know everything there is to know about it,* I reasoned, *then maybe I can finally stop thinking about it.* But I was unable to access any of the newspaper files from that year.

"That's strange," the librarian said when I called to ask for help. "All newspaper accounts from that year appear to be deleted from the central computer. Even the backup files are gone."

I figured it was a fluke until I discovered all the Mills family photos were missing from our computer file. If not for Rita's diary, there would be no evidence that the Mills family ever existed.

13

"WHY WOULD SOMEONE WANT TO ERASE MY PAST?"
I asked Kyle. It was Wednesday afternoon and he had
stopped by after school to take me to Twin-Star Labs
for more tests.

"Maybe it was a computer glitch," he suggested as
we pulled out of my driveway.

"I don't think so," I said. I rolled down my window.
My eyes felt small and gritty, and I couldn't stop
yawning. I'd slept very little the last couple of nights
and my tiredness was catching up with me. As the car
picked up speed, a crisp breeze rushed through the
window, refreshing me. It slid coolly over my face,
blowing back my hair.

"Computers aren't infallible," Kyle said.

"Why did my family photos *and* the newspaper
files on my sister's murder disappear at the same

time? It's too much of a coincidence! Someone came into my house and erased everything, and then they went to the library and did the same thing."

He regarded me skeptically. "Why would anyone do that?"

"That's what I'd like to know! All I know is *someone* was in my house. My neighbor saw him running away. He must have been watching the house and came back when I left to—"

I let the rest of the sentence hang. I didn't want to tell Kyle about my visit to my brother. He would never understand why I felt such a connection to Jim.

"Your neighbor saw the burglar? What did he look like?"

"Ruby didn't get a good look at him. She said it could have been a man or a woman."

"Maybe it was Suki. She's a weird girl. Didn't you say she was always stealing stuff from you?"

"Yes," I conceded. "She's stolen some of my makeup, but this is different. Why would she mess with my computer?"

"Why would *anyone*? This whole thing is crazy, Jenna. My theory about Suki makes as much sense as anything else."

He was right. Maybe Suki *did* erase my past. Maybe she was jealous because I knew more about my history than she knew about hers. She'd seemed so sad when she told me all she had left of her mother was three photographs. But she'd made such a point of wanting to help me "re-create" my family in the VR program. Was that just an act?

Suki was strange. Still, I could not believe she'd be that cruel. My gut feeling said someone else had erased my family history—someone who wanted to harm me.

Something evil is in the air. It's all around us, closing in, and I don't know what to do. I shivered, remembering Rita's words. No one believed she was in danger—until it was too late. Was *I* in danger? Or was I only imagining things because I was spooked by what had happened to Rita?

With my mind so cluttered, it was harder than usual concentrating on Dr. Grady's rambling monologues. When he pulled out the visor, I perked up. Though my powers scared me, I admit I was intrigued.

Kyle asked to sit in on my session, and when he saw the visor, he grinned at me, his face flushed in excitement.

"You're ready for the next big step, Jenna," Dr. Grady said. "As I explained earlier, the visor is fueled with a PK enforcing substance. When I flick the visor's 'on' switch, the inner tubes heat to 120 degrees. In cooler temperatures the fuel is dormant, but the heat brings the fuel to an active state. The visor's fuel will pull the PK energy from your brain waves and circulate it back through, strengthening it."

I slipped the visor over my head. The instant I turned it on, it grew warm. It felt natural, as if it were a part of me. Energy—in the form of crackling, blue rays of light—shot from my eyes. Instantaneously, the energy circled back to an area above my ears and into my mind. It was an odd, tingling sensation that left me heady with power.

"Let's see what you can do with this," Dr. Grady said and placed a tall, green bottle behind a Plexiglas screen.

I stared at the bottle, imagining it blowing apart into a million pieces. I channeled all my energy—my anger, frustration, and fear—into the rays aimed at the bottle. The blue rays washed over it, but it remained intact.

"Focus, Jenna," Dr. Grady urged. "*Focus!*"

I concentrated harder and the rays deepened with the intensity of my thoughts, finally darkening to midnight-blue as my mind seemed to hum. Then, suddenly, the bottle exploded with a bang, sending sharp sprays of glass to the corners of the room.

I leapt back, startled to see I'd actually done it.

"Not bad," Dr. Grady said. "Two minutes and forty-five seconds." He tried to sound casual, but there was a breathlessness to his usually gruff voice.

I discovered I could control the dice ninety percent of the time while wearing the visor. And in just two minutes, I twisted a paper clip into a knot. After forty minutes of PK exercises, I was mentally drained and the visor was nearly empty. As the fuel ran low, my abilities weakened.

"That's enough for today, Jenna," Dr. Grady said, reaching for the visor. I flinched as his fingers brushed my hair. His touch made my flesh crawl.

"We must be conservative with the fuel," he cautioned. "It's mixed from several rare substances.

Every drop is expensive and hard to come by. Obviously, you're exhausted, and therefore using the fuel at a faster rate. We'll experiment again tomorrow when you're rested."

His assumptive attitude annoyed me. He thought he could snap his fingers and I'd obey.

"What if I'm *busy* tomorrow?" I said coolly and glared at him.

He pretended not to notice my resentment, but his eyes flickered darkly. He smiled stiffly and asked, "What day would be convenient for you, Jenna?"

"I've got lots of homework," I said. "I'll call you when I get some free time."

I didn't really have much homework. The truth is, I was anxious to wear the visor again. But I was *more* anxious to take control of my life. So far, the scientists had made all the decisions for me. They'd suspended me on ice for a century and chosen my birth time as casually as they would plan an office party. It was *their* fault I was born in the wrong time—*their* fault I'd never know my real family!

In this day and age, animal experiments were illegal. Yet *I* felt like the proverbial guinea pig. *No more!* If I helped with the experiments, it would be on my terms.

If.

I hadn't made up my mind if I was going to continue working with Twin-Star. My biological parents had signed a contract with Twin-Star. But I had rights. I was pretty sure the scientists couldn't force me to do anything I didn't want to.

I toyed with the idea of telling Dr. Grady I had no intention of returning—no intention of ever wearing the visor again. Then Kyle smiled at me. "You were great, Jenna!" he whispered. "Really great!"

I melted as his shining eyes held mine. The PK experiments were so important to him—a tribute to the grandfather he adored. Involuntarily, my lips curved into a smile as wide as Kyle's.

"I wish my grandfather was alive to see this," he said proudly.

In that instant, I made a decision. I would help with the experiments. But I'd make it clear to everyone it was *my* choice. "I've got some time Saturday," I told Dr. Grady. "I could come in for a while in the afternoon."

I told myself I was doing it for Kyle. After all, what difference did it make to me how many knots I could tie in a fork with my mind waves? I could see no practical application for my newfound talent. The one time I'd tried to use it outside the lab, someone had gotten hurt. Whenever I saw Ruby hobbling around with her walker, I felt a fresh wave of guilt.

But my guilt, my doubt, and my gnawing sense of foreboding were whisked away with Kyle's kisses. When he dropped me off, he held me close. As his lips gently brushed mine, I felt a surge of emotion I was sure must be love. I wanted to make him happy, and I silently vowed to do my best on Saturday.

On Saturday, everything changed. My drive to succeed had nothing to do with Kyle or Dr. Grady or any of the scientists at Twin-Star Labs. You see, I discovered the reason behind the PK experiments. It was a theory so fantastic, it seemed impossible. But if it proved true, I could right the terrible wrong that had been done to me.

14

IT WAS THOUGHTS OF RITA THAT LED ME TO THE truth. She was constantly on my mind. When I looked in the mirror, I imagined *her* eyes staring back at me. At night I dreamed of her. Vivid dreams that seemed to fill every second of my slumber.

The dreams usually started happily. Rita and I would find each other and she would instantly recognize me as her sister. Ecstatic, we'd laugh and skip like children. We'd frolic over rolling hills, dance under rainbows, and bounce on pink, fluffy clouds.

But always the dream lost its soft fairyland quality, sharpening and distorting until it twisted itself into a grotesque nightmare. Rainbows turned black and clouds wept blood. Rita became a skeleton, rattling her bones as she danced away from me.

"Rita!" I shrieked. "Come back!"

"I can't, Jenna," she replied. "Can't you see I'm dead?"

The awful dreams left me sick and anxious.

You'd think I'd want to forget her, to shove all thoughts of her from my mind. Rita's life had ended so tragically. What was the point of dwelling on it?

Yet, I made no effort to forget my sister. On the contrary. I ached to know all I could about her. I slept in her room, strolled on her beach, stared at the same stars that sprinkled her sky. Still, it was not enough.

Listening to Rita's music partly filled the void. On Saturday afternoon, when my parents were away visiting friends in Salem, I programmed our computer to play the melodies my sister was so fond of. I could hardly wait for Mom and Dad to leave so I could have the house to myself. But Mom had dawdled, watering the plants and changing her outfit three times, and then had practically *begged* me to go with them. "Please come with us, Jen-Jen," she asked with annoying cheerfulness.

I cringed at my childhood nickname—the corny, gooey name she gave me as a baby. *I'm not your Jen-Jen!* I wanted to shout. Instead, I said stiffly, "I've got things to do."

"Your homework will still be here when you get back. The Halversons would love to see you! You haven't seen Sheila in over three years. You two girls were so cute together when you were little," she gushed, her eyes focused in that faraway, sentimental way she gets when she reminisces. "I remember when Marnie and I used to bathe you girls together. You had a little blue plastic tugboat you named Betsy. You took it in the tub with you and —"

Her words died as she noticed my cold stare.

"Thank you for inviting me," I said with icy politeness. "But I really have things to do. Dr. Grady is expecting me at the lab this afternoon."

Dad slipped a sweater over Mom's shoulders and warned, "We're going to be late, Esther." To me he said, "We're proud of you for sticking with your commitments."

Then he ushered Mom out the door, and I hardened myself against the last pleading glance she'd thrown me, pain skittering across her violet eyes.

Did she think she could win me over with sugary memories of my babyhood? Was that her way of convincing me everything was okay? If anything, her reminiscing had the opposite effect. It only served to remind me it had all been a lie. That she was simply pretending to be the person she wasn't. My mother.

I had spent the first seventeen years of my life living the lie she'd spun for me. Now, it was time to learn about the real me, my *real* family. *My sister!* And so I programmed the computer to pour out Rita's music.

The old music was so different from the music I was accustomed to. It was startling to hear actual voices of real human beings singing to me—such a far cry from the perfectly pitched computerized voices of the twenty-first century music!

At first the bands with such silly names—The Beatles, The Moody Blues, Led Zeppelin—seemed quaint and sweet and ridiculously old-fashioned. But as I listened I heard stories and messages and warnings in the strange lyrics. My mind drifted with the haunting voices and my feet tapped involuntarily to the music's beat.

"What is that *noise*?" Kyle asked when he came to pick me up to take me to the lab.

I grabbed his hand and danced him into our living room. "It's The Beatles!" I said. "Kids listened to this music almost a century ago!"

He laughed. "It sounds weird."

"It grows on you after a while," I said. "Kids back then didn't have Tune-Chips and they *liked* sharing their musical experiences with each other. I've been reading about a rock festival called Woodstock. My sister went to it with her cousins in 1969. Half a million people showed up! Imagine all those people groovin' to the same beat!"

"Groovin'?" Kyle repeated scornfully. "You sound like my grandma!"

"That's the way kids talked back then," I said defensively. "Anyway, Woodstock lasted for three days, and it started raining and everyone was sloshing around in the mud helping each other because they were into peace and brotherhood and—"

"What a bunch of spards!" he interrupted. "I'd hate to wallow in the mud with a crowd of strangers listening to weird music."

"But it was *different* back then! People were into the earth and each other and—"

My words trailed away as Kyle's mouth flattened

into a grim line. "I thought you were going to put all that stuff about the past behind you, Jenna."

"I'm just listening to old music. What's wrong with that?"

"It's like you're *obsessed*! I'm worried about you."

Touched by his concern, I said gently, "I just think this old music is interesting. That's all."

He plopped down on our couch and said, "I hope you mean that, because I've been feeling kind of bad about what happened to you. That's got to be a real mind twister to find out you were on ice for a hundred years."

"It is," I said flatly.

"I thought maybe you'd blame me because my family owns an interest in Twin-Star," he confessed, ducking his head to avoid my gaze.

Taken aback by his sudden show of sensitivity, I sat silent for a moment, searching for the right words. "This isn't your fault, Kyle," I finally said. "I blame the adults—the scientists and my parents. They're the ones who did this to me. You weren't even born when they decided to plant me in Mom—let alone when they *froze* me!"

He smiled weakly. "You seemed upset at the last session with Dr. Grady. If you want to quit the experiments I'll understand."

"I thought you were excited about this! Your grandfather invented the visor and you're helping to carry on his work. I thought it was important to you—"

"It *is*! I was close to my grandfather. It means a lot to see his work continued. But not if it hurts you."

I sank onto the couch beside him. "I know sometimes I act like I have brain-drag, but that's just because I get moody," I said. "I *want* to help with the
visor experiments."

It would have been a relief to unload on someone,
to express how terrible, how disoriented, how *lonely* I
felt.

But Kyle already felt bad. There was no point in
making him feel worse. As I smiled brightly, insisting
I was excited about the experiments, my only goal
was to make my new boyfriend happy.

I, however, still mistakenly believed the visor held
no special significance for me. I did not guess the scientists were keeping yet *another* secret from me.

But with Rita forever on the edge of my thoughts, I
was soon to discover the truth. It started out as a rou-
tine experiment. Dr. Grady and I were alone in the
lab. He handed me the visor and placed a sealed cardboard box on the table.

"What's inside?" I asked.

"A paper clip."

I was disappointed. I figured I'd graduated beyond
bending paper clips and was ready for something
more exciting.

"I want you to transport it to my office," he said.

I stared at him.

"There's a sealed empty box on my desk," he explained. "It is identical to this one." He picked up the
box and shook it. The paper clip bounced softly
against the cardboard. "Visualize it. Concentrate on
transporting this paper clip to the empty box."

"How?"

"*Your* mind holds that secret, Jenna. Do it. Do it the way you've accomplished every other task we've asked you to."

"But is it possible?" I asked, and then remembered the boy who had transported his teddy bear across the country. And my sister who had made a paper clip vanish. Did it really vanish? Or did she transport it to another place?

I flicked on the visor and stared at the box. *Rita did it! I can too!* The thought hung there, between me and the box. I tried to erase it, for I'd learned that PK exercises are most successful without words. Thoughts just seem to clutter the air. And the air must be clear of all but what I want to accomplish. I tried to empty my mind.

Rita did it!

It wasn't working. I could not concentrate on transporting the paper clip. All I could think of was Rita's paper clip.

Rita did it!

The blue rays poured from my eyes and rippled over the box, flowing like punch. I was wasting the visor's precious fuel. I was about to admit that this exercise was too complicated when the rays suddenly flared into an orange light. A loud pop followed. For an instant, it seemed I'd set the box afire. Then the orange faded back to blue. The box was still intact. I turned off the visor.

"Something happened," I said.

Dr. Grady picked up the box and rattled it.

"It's still there," I said, shrugging my shoulders apologetically. "My mind's not on this today."

"It sounds different," he said, shaking the box again. It made a tinkling sound, like metal on metal.

He ripped open the box. The paper clip was still there. Beside it was a *second* paper clip, its edge smudged with white paint.

"Where did *that* come from?" I asked.

Dr. Grady's eyes gleamed as he stared at it. "This is incredible," he gasped.

"What? What happened?"

When he hesitated, I snapped, "I have a right to know!"

"I have no intention of keeping anything from you," he said evenly. "Something quite remarkable has occurred, confirming all we've been working toward. If I'm not mistaken, this paper clip was sent here by your sister."

"*What?*"

"We can't keep you in the dark any longer. It's important you understand the reason for the experiments if you are to successfully aid us."

"How many more secrets do you have?" I asked, bristling.

"We never intentionally kept secrets from you. It's just that some of the facts are difficult to comprehend. We didn't want to overwhelm you with too much too soon."

"Just tell me what's going on!"

He set the paper clip on the desk and looked me in the eye. "We've been trying to crack time barriers," he said. "That is the whole purpose behind the visor. For decades, our research has indicated that telekinetic energy transcends the tangible laws that apply to matter. Your unique PK skills, when combined with the visor, result in an ability to create time warps. Tell me something, Jenna. Were you thinking about Rita's disappearing paper clip a moment ago?"

"Yes. I tried to concentrate on moving the paper clip like you asked me to, but I kept thinking about Rita and what she did to her paper clip."

"I suspected as much. A century ago, in a controlled laboratory experiment, Rita sent this paper clip on a journey. Apparently, you zeroed in on it and caused it to materialize here."

I barely had a chance to comprehend this new development before Dr. Grady led me to his office and asked me to try something new.

"Visualize a later time in the day—let's say around five p.m.," he said. "It's 1:15 now. Try to transport yourself to this room at five."

It was an incredible request. The thing he was so matter-of-factly proposing was impossible. He might as well have asked me to sprout apples from my fingertips. I wanted to ask him how I was supposed to accomplish such a thing, but I could already hear his standard response: "*Your* mind holds the key, Jenna."

Perhaps it did. When I thought of the things I'd done these past days, anything seemed possible. So I sank into Dr. Grady's cushiony chair, turned on the visor, and tried to do what he asked of me. As the rays shot from my pupils and my head seemed to vibrate beneath the visor, I imagined my mind held a clock and I pictured the hands of that clock sweeping round and round until they rested at five.

When I glanced at Dr. Grady's desk clock, I was surprised to see it was 5:06. He was no longer in the room, but Tarynn was there, watering the plants.

"Tarynn, are you busy?" the receptionist called over the intercom.

"I'm almost done with the plants," she answered.

"Somebody named Daniel is on the phone. He wants to know what time he should pick you up. He's real cute!"

Tarynn smiled. "Don't get any ideas. This is our second date and I think it's getting serious."

She reached past me—rather rudely, I thought— and punched a button on Dr. Grady's telephone so the face of a young, bearded man appeared on the telephone screen.

Then she sat down—on *me*! That's when I realized she couldn't see or feel me, because I could not feel her. I was not there. My *mind* was. It was as if I was having some sort of psychic vision.

As Tarynn chatted with her boyfriend, a sharp sheet of hail pelted the window.

"Jenna, can you hear me?" Dr. Grady called. "Are you alright? *Jenna!*"

Suddenly, the room spun out of focus and when it slowed again I was staring up into Dr. Grady's anxious face. "You were in some kind of trance."

"I *did* it!" I gasped. "I was here at 5:06 and Tarynn was watering the plants and then this guy called."

His eyes narrowed skeptically. "You didn't go anywhere."

"I *did*!" I insisted. "His name was Daniel. Tarynn sat right here in this chair and talked to him on your phone."

Dr. Grady sighed. "You've been accomplishing great things. But I asked you to do too much too soon. I had hoped you could actually transport yourself through time, and I give you credit for trying. But the fact is, you weren't able to do it."

"You think I'm *lying*?" I asked, indignant.

"You wanted to believe you could accomplish what I requested, and you simply convinced yourself you had."

He had asked me to do the impossible and somehow I'd done it. Now he didn't believe me! Angrily, I snapped, "I didn't imagine it. It was *real*!"

He looked thoughtful. "Alright then. Tell me everything you saw and heard."

I described the hail hitting the window and Tarynn's phone conversation. He didn't bother to write anything down, and I was beginning to suspect that the hidden video cameras my father had told me about were everywhere in Twin-Star, recording everything all the time.

Dr. Grady confirmed that suspicion during my next session, the following Saturday. "I owe you an apology," he said, not sounding the least sorry. His hidden office camera, he informed me, had taped Tarynn watering his plants at 5:06. It also caught her conversation with Daniel and the hail beating on the window.

"The visor committee has thoroughly studied the incident and we've concluded you projected your mind through time," he said. "We had not previously considered the possibility of a mind-body separation in connection with time travel. That is why I initially doubted your claim. But the videotape of Tarynn substantiates everything you said. With a little more practice, we believe you may be capable of moving your entire being."

"You mean *time travel*? Like they do in stories?"

"We certainly have every indication that you will accomplish what scientists have only dreamed of for centuries. We now have the technology to amplify your PK skills, making it possible for you to travel into the future."

"If I can go into the future," I asked, "can I also go into the past?"

"If that were feasible, we'd be inundated with tourists from the future."

"It doesn't make sense," I argued. "If I can move forward in time, why not backward?"

"It may be possible," he admitted. "But we're looking at an ethical question here. If someone actually traveled into the past, it could have devastating repercussions on the present."

"How?"

Dr. Grady leaned back in his chair and forced a smile as if he were trying to look patient. "If you were to visit the past, you might do something that seems insignificant to you that could affect the future as it was meant to be," he said slowly. "A minor thing could set off a long chain of events. For instance, let's say on your trip to the past, you went into a restaurant and ordered a glass of orange juice. Suppose that orange juice was the last glass left. The next customer comes in, orders a glass of orange juice but is disappointed to learn it's all gone. He leaves and as a result never meets the woman who arrives five minutes later. If he'd met her, he would have married her and fathered her child. That child would have become the president of the United States."

"Maybe their child would have been a psychopathic *killer*," I said. "Then the trip to the past would have been a good thing."

He shook his head. "It's dangerous, Jenna. Don't even entertain the idea. My belief is that future generations have vowed to never travel back into our time—although they probably have the means to do it. They know coming here would be a threat to their current existence. You must never even think about upsetting the natural order of things."

Upsetting the natural order of things? I thought angrily. *That's what the scientists did to me when they yanked me from my rightful century!*

Despite Dr. Grady's warnings, I made a decision. I would try to go back in time, and if I could, I knew exactly what I would do. I would stop my sister's murderer.

15

DEAR DIARY,

A moment ago, the phone rang. I ran out to the hallway to answer it. I knew somebody was on the line, because I heard them breathing, but they didn't say anything. I got that icy feeling again, as if something bad was going to happen! I slammed down the phone, came back in here, and huddled up on my window seat to write in you.

Maybe it was just a crank call, Diary, but my hands are shaking so bad that my words are spilling from my pen in squiggly lines. Now my favorite song just came on the radio, "Crystal Blue Persuasion" by Tommy James and the Shondells. It is calming me as I sing along and you'll notice that my handwriting is getting easier to read. The song is lifting me! I will write

some of the words here, perhaps they hold an answer
for me. "The sun is arising, most definitely . . .

". . . LOVE IS THE ANSWER."

Yes, Diary! I do believe that. Love IS the answer.
But what is the question???

It was Sunday afternoon, and once again my sister's diary held me riveted. I leaned back in my window seat and answered the question she'd punctuated
with triple question marks.

"The question," I said, "is *how* can I save you?
How can I get the visor to work so I can go back and
help you?"

"LOVE IS THE ANSWER."

I stared at the purple capital letters she'd underlined
several times as she reiterated a line in the song. It
was as if she was answering *my* question. Love *was*
the answer to the question of how I would save her!

If I could truly love my sister, it would immerse me
in thoughts of her. And once those thoughts were
sharp and clear, I would have the concentration necessary to transport myself back to her.

Clear sharp thoughts! That was the key to moving
myself against the impossible walls of time.

I asked my computer to play, "Crystal Blue Persuasion."

It was a clean melody with a light background of
drums and the sweet strumming of guitar strings that
sliced to my soul. Rife with messages about peace and
brotherhood, "Crystal Blue Persuasion" also seemed
to have a *special* message just for me.

I closed my eyes and let the music carry me. *"Love.*

Love is the answer. And that's alright. So don't you give up now . . ."

Was the song talking to me? Urging me not to give up on saving my sister? I shivered.

". . . Look to your soul and open your mind."

Open my mind? That was exactly what I needed to do to get the visor to work.

As I read Rita's thoughts, I vowed to concentrate so intensely on her that she would become crystal clear in my mind—so clear I could transport myself to her side.

Diary, my favorite song is over now and an obnoxious disc jockey is telling stupid jokes so I'm going to turn off the radio.

I'm back. Now it is quiet—TOO QUIET! It frightens me. Last night I had a nightmare. Cruel hands closed around my throat and I couldn't breathe. What does it mean? Perhaps it is only symbolic and I am feeling suffocated by school, my mother's restrictions, and all the other walls in my life.

Diary, I wish I could believe that is all it is. But there's a shadow over me. I tried to talk to April about it when my parents wouldn't listen. She said she gets depressed too and not to worry because it will pass. She does not understand! I have a premonition something awful will happen soon but I don't know what! No one will listen! Why won't anybody help me?

"*I* will, Rita," I said. "I'll do everything in my power to help you!"

In the next weeks, I threw myself into the PK experiments with an intensity that left me exhausted.

And I became increasingly proficient at using the visor.

Dr. Grady assisted me in more short time journeys. They began calling these time trips "mind projections," because my body never moved.

The scientists would ask me to visualize a later time—never more than a few days into the future, and I'd slip into a sort of trance and project my mind to a destination. Afterward, they would record my observations.

The more fuel in the visor, the stronger my capabilities. We also discovered it was easiest for me to project myself to the same location I started from. For instance, if I was in Dr. Grady's office, I'd project myself to a later time in his office, rather than to one of the labs.

I let the scientists believe I cared about the experiments for the experiments themselves. But I was biding my time, learning all I could. Foremost in my mind was the thought of saving my sister—and of going back to the time where I belonged. Where I was meant to be, before Twin-Star Labs had interfered.

Without Dr. Grady's knowledge, I began changing the experiments. Before going a day into the future, I'd project my mind into the *past*. I'd go to yesterday, but before returning, I'd make a quick trip to *tomorrow* so I'd have something to tell Dr. Grady.

Though encouraged by my progress, I was also frustrated. I wanted to do more than simply project my mind. Even if my mind could project back to

1970, what good would it do Rita if all I could do was observe her murder?

To stop my sister's killer, it was necessary to *physically* transport myself back to her time. But the scientists were moving painstakingly slow on the project. Satisfied with the mind projections, Dr. Grady seemed in no hurry for me to transport my body through time.

So far, all I'd done was project my mind a few days into the past or a few days into the future. I wasn't even sure if it was possible to do any full-fledged time traveling. Yet, I needed to *try*.

But throughout the experiments, the scientists were always hovering around, scrutinizing and recording everything. I was afraid to attempt to time travel with them watching me. What if I failed? They might discover my plan and prevent me from ever trying it again.

One blustery November afternoon, an unexpected opportunity presented itself. The visor had just been filled, my mind was clear, and Dr. Grady had left me and Kyle alone in his office while he went to confer with another scientist.

I did not want to betray Kyle. Yet my sister needed me, and there might not be another chance to help her.

"I'm thirsty," I said, fingering the visor on Dr. Grady's desk. "I can't concentrate when I'm thirsty."

"I'll get you some water," Kyle offered, crossing the room to the beverage dispenser. "Or would you rather have juice?"

"I'd really like a Purple Fizzy," I said. "With lots of ice!"

Dr. Grady's dispenser had not been stocked with Fizzies. The Fizzy machine was down a long hallway and two floors up. But Kyle grinned obligingly—as I knew he would—and headed out the door toward the Fizzy machine.

I felt a sudden sharp tug of regret as he jovially called over his shoulder, "One Purple Fizzy, extra ice, coming right up!"

I would not be there when he returned. I would not see the surprise in his trusting green eyes, followed by shock when he realized he'd been deceived.

When Kyle's tall frame disappeared through the doorway, I counted to ten, tucked the visor under my jacket, and hurried into the hallway. Nervously, I glanced down the long, stark hall that led to the receptionist's desk.

"Hi, Jenna," a cheerful voice said. "Are you done already?"

I spun around to see Tarynn emerging from the ladies' room.

"I was just going to get a Fizzy," I stammered. A hot flush crawled up my neck as Tarynn's eyes slid to the bulge under my jacket.

"The machine's the other way," she said suspiciously.

"I know. I was just going to see something in the lobby first."

She nodded as if she understood, but her eyes burned into my back as I hurried down the hall.

By the time I reached the receptionist's desk, I was running. The alarm began shrieking just as I flew through the front door. Perhaps it was Tarynn who alerted security, or maybe they'd seen me on their hidden cameras. It didn't matter. *They were on to me*.

I'd counted on a full five-minute head start—just enough time to catch the solar-bus around the corner and make my escape.

But with the alarm blaring, I knew security would burst out the door at any moment. There was nothing to do but flee. I dashed across the parking lot, a cold, wet wind scalding my face. I dropped to my knees behind a row of shiny solar-mobiles and crawled along the rough pavement. From this vantage point, I saw several pairs of legs, clad in the bright orange of the security uniforms.

"She couldn't have gotten far," a strident female voice exclaimed. "Jane, you go that way! Maurice, you take the east lot, and I'll cover the front."

The three pairs of legs raced off in opposite directions while I crouched behind a car, my heartbeat thundering in my ears. For a moment, it seemed they were all moving away from me, but then footsteps approached.

I inched beneath a car, silently praying they wouldn't find me. Nausea swept through me as the sharp scent of oil and asphalt rolled up from the pavement and filled my lungs.

The footsteps slowed as they neared, finally stopping directly in front of my hiding place. A hand reached down and closed around my wrist and a familiar voice hissed, "Hurry, Jenna!"

I looked up at Suki, her eyes wide and frightened.

"I've got the keys to my uncle's car," she said. "*Hurry* before they see you!"

A moment later, I was hunched on the floor on Dr. Grady's solar-mobile as Suki drove from the parking lot, tires squealing.

"I know what you're planning," she said. "If it works for you, I want to go back too. I want to meet my mother!"

"How did you know?" I asked.

"I'm a little psychic like my mother was. I could see in your eyes you were planning something. I've been helping Uncle Terry at the lab and overheard him talking about the time travel experiments. I knew what I'd do if I were in your shoes—if I had as much PK ability as you."

She was the only one who understood.

"I was looking out the window and saw you leave," she said. "I followed the security guards outside."

Suki agreed to take me home. It was the one place I could be certain existed in 1970. "It will be easiest to transport from there," I said.

She nodded. "Go to the attic. That way you won't startle the Mills family by suddenly appearing in their living room. No one's likely to be in the attic when you arrive."

"Good idea. I don't know how to thank—"

"Promise me one thing!" Suki begged. "Find my mother. Tell her I forgive her. Her name was Trudy Calacort and she was a professional tarot card reader."

Suki had made it sound so easy. But I knew the chances of success were slim. There was no way to gauge just how far the visor's fuel would carry me. A year? Ten years? Thirty years? None of those destinations would do me a bit of good. Wherever I ended up, it was possible I'd deplete the visor's fuel, preventing me from ever returning.

If I pondered the consequences, my courage would dissolve. So I slipped on the visor and visualized my sister. *Rita, you are my flesh and blood!* The thought was so intense it seemed to squeeze my mind.

"Love is the answer." Blue rays darted from the visor, vibrating my skull as they circled back through my brain.

March, 1970. A party on the beach. My sister laughing. The words crystallized into pictures and I embraced them, imagining myself by Rita's side.

Back where I belong . . .

My head began to ache and I welcomed the pain. The pain was a sort of energy and I seized it, focusing it through the visor. *Rita!*

My thoughts were screaming and my mind turned inside out. Suddenly, my body felt numb. Ferocious, churning clouds scuttled past the attic window. In the next instant the sun burst through and then bright snowflakes glided past the glass. The weather changed rapidly and dramatically, a process that repeated itself in an endless succession as I experienced the sensation of being sucked into a vacuum.

Voices filled the attic—laughing, crying, shouting, whispering, reminiscing—they passed over me in jumbled layers, like the voices of ghosts from the past.

Snatches of garbled attic conversation floated over me: ". . . old prom dress still fits . . ." ". . . No one's up here, so it must have been mice . . ." ". . . can't believe moths ate Eddie's baby blanket . . ."

The eerie voices finally melted into silence and everything grew still. Except for my throbbing headache, I felt no different. Nothing had changed. I had failed.

I lay looking up at the slanted ceiling of the attic. How long until Dr. Grady found me? What would he do to me when he did?

Maybe I should just turn myself in. I picked myself up from the wooden floor and dusted off my pants.

"Meow."

Startled, I turned to see a fat yellow cat curled in a box of papers under the window.

"Where did you come from?" I asked. Turning slowly, I appraised the unfamiliar items that now cluttered the attic: an array of women's wigs perched atop a row of styrofoam heads, a dusty wooden chair with a missing leg, a tall, amateurish painting of a girl in a long dress. None of these had been there before.

The rusty bicycle was gone, replaced by a cardboard box overflowing with shiny red Christmas balls.

I darted to the window, my heart skipping. I craned my neck, turning my head to the south. Ruby's home was gone! A square white house squatted in its place. A young mother sat on the porch. Dressed in old-fashioned denim shorts and halter top, she bounced a plump baby on her knee. As I watched, she gently placed the baby in a playpen, picked up a paintbrush, and began painting the house's shutters a sunshiny yellow. It was like watching an old movie of a time gone by. For a moment, I forgot to breathe as my eyes followed the careful strokes of the paintbrush. Eventually, I came out of my daze and took in the whole picture—the old-fashioned stop sign, the unfamiliar patch of scraggly vegetable garden, and the car resembling a museum relic parked in the driveway.

I'd done it! I'd actually traveled back in time!

Had I traveled to the right time? I pressed my forehead to the glass, scanning the yard. The maple tree barely reached the attic window. Only moments before, its gnarly branches had stretched past the rooftop.

Suddenly shouts and laughter sliced the silence as several teenage boys raced across the grassy backyard, headed toward the beach path. With cold dread, I recognized the one with shaggy black hair and stocky frame. *Ben!*

Were they headed to one of those beer parties on the beach? "Keggers," Rita had called them.

Was this the night Ben would hurt my sister?

As I stared out the window, every muscle taut with terror, something horrible occurred to me. In my rush to escape, I'd forgotten something so incredibly important I wanted to cry.

I'd neglected to check the date of Rita's murder. If I

remembered correctly, she'd died in March but I could not recall the day.

Without such vital information, how could I save my sister?

16

FOR A FLEETING INSTANT, I CONSIDERED RETURNING
to 2070 where I could get organized and come back to
1970 fully prepared. But there was no guarantee the
visor held enough fuel for a hundred-year round-trip.
In fact, I might not be able to return to 2070. I could
end up halfway home, in some obscure place like the
year 2020 where I couldn't relate to anybody. Stuck
there forever!

Even if I had enough fuel, it didn't mean I'd be *capable* of traveling through time again. This trip might
have been a fluke. I wasn't even sure how I'd accomplished it.

This could very well be my only chance to help
Rita.

How could I stop Ben from hurting her? As my

eyes wandered over the collection of wigs, an idea came to me. What if I broke them up?

According to my sister's diary, a blonde had enticed Ben away from her once before. Why not again? Obviously, he liked blondes. I could wear the blond wig and lure him away from Rita. If I could keep them apart for that night, it would give me time to think of a long-term plan.

I chose a wig with straight, lemony locks that fell to my shoulders. It fit tightly, smelled musty, and made my neck itch. After adding a pair of round, orange-tinted sunglasses, I was somewhat disguised.

I surveyed myself in the tall mirror that was propped in the attic corner. From the neck up, I looked okay. But my puff-suit would not do!

A search of the attic for more appropriate clothes turned up only a yellowing wedding gown and a box of baby clothes.

The sun had slipped low in the sky, its rays filtering weakly through the dusty window. Banbury Bay's waves glittered and winked in the soft, gold light. Soon it would be dusk. Night would follow, slithering in to coat the beach in darkness and hide a killer's crimes.

"Hang on, Rita!" I whispered, frantic to get to her.

One place in that house was certain to have the right clothes. *Rita's room!*

I hid my visor behind the old trunk in the corner, slowly opened the attic door, and peeked into the hallway below. The house was still, as if holding its breath, waiting for the family to return. The cat leapt from the box, startling me as he brushed between my ankles. He looked back at me once, green eyes blinking drowsily, and bounded down the stairs.

I half expected to find Rita stretched out on her bed, listening to music and scribbling in her diary. But the room was empty. My antique maple dresser sat between the windows, and Rita's unmade bed was parked against the wall in the same exact place as mine. That's where the decorating resemblance ended.

Rita's walls were blue and covered with posters of long-haired young men clutching guitars, waifs with gigantic dark eyes, and a cartoon man with a big nose and huge brown shoes with a balloon coming from his mouth that said, "Keep on Truckin'."

A square of shaggy green carpet covered the floor, and a boxy record player sat in the corner. Ignoring the clothes heaped on Rita's bed, I headed for her closet. Wire hangers jingled tunelessly as I reached into the depths of the closet, searching for something Rita rarely wore and might not recognize. I found it at the back of the closet—a pale yellow button-up sweater she'd apparently outgrown. It fit me snugly but would have to do. A pair of Rita's jeans and sneakers completed my outfit.

Three breathless minutes later, I was racing down the dirt path. Nearly a hundred teenagers swarmed the beach, but I spotted Benjamin Grand instantly. He stood by a big silver keg that was perched on a log. I slipped up behind him, watching as he opened the tap and filled his cup. The beer flowed too fast and his cup foamed over. He tipped it, drinking greedily, ignoring the fact he'd left the tap open.

"Hey, Grand!" a frizzy-haired guy shouted. "Watch what you're doing! You're wasting beer!"

Someone turned off the tap, as an oblivious Ben swayed unsteadily and stared toward the water through glassy red eyes.

"Grand's wasted," someone said and chortled.

He *was* out of it. Really drunk. Drunk enough to kill?

I wasn't taking any chances with my sister's life. I had to get Ben as far away from Rita's house as possible.

"Hi, Ben," I gushed, touching his elbow and smiling flirtatiously. I'd never taken acting classes and hadn't had much practice lying, but I managed to slather it on pretty thick. "You probably don't remember me, but we met at a party last summer," I said.

"What's your name?" he slurred and tried to fix his watery blue eyes on me.

"I'm Kathy." I forced a lighthearted giggle. "A friend of mine wants to ask you something. She's waiting down the beach."

"Tell her to come join the party."

"She broke her leg and is in a cast." I looped my arm in his. "She can't walk very well, Ben. She really needs to talk to you."

Obediently, he fell into step beside me and we headed south along the shore. I hadn't allowed myself to contemplate the consequences of enticing a killer down a deserted stretch of beach. Perhaps if I'd considered my own safety, I would have found another strategy. But my mind was still whirling from that impossible trip through time.

The sun slid toward the faraway islands as we trudged along the shore. The last rays of the day burned the sky in a brilliant orange light that seemed to set the clouds on fire.

I paused, marveling at the incredible fact I could stand there and enjoy the beauty of a sunset that had graced the sky nearly a century before I was born.

"So where's your friend?" Ben asked. He tossed the empty cup in the waves and pulled a fresh can of beer from the pocket of his jean jacket.

"It's not far now," I said quickly.

We'd rounded the bend and the party sounds had faded. *I was alone with a killer.* Would anyone hear me if I screamed?

"What did you say your name was?" Ben asked.

"Karen," I said, realizing too late I'd told him Kathy before. He didn't notice.

"You do look familiar."

If he hadn't been so loaded, he surely would have known why. I looked just like his girlfriend—except for my blond wig.

Ben's long stride lacked coordination as he lurched along beside me, occasionally stepping into the water. The alcohol had made him clumsy, but he was still strong. His huge hand closed menacingly around the empty beer can, crumpling it into a tight little ball.

I shuddered and skipped a few steps ahead. We'd traveled about a quarter of a mile down the beach and

I wasn't sure what to do next. My only plan had been to lead Ben away from Rita's territory. What would he do if he discovered my lie?

I suspected he'd be angry. I knew Benjamin Grand got violent when he was angry. The shrill breathlessness of my own voice surprised me as I said, "My friend is around here someplace!"

Ben pulled another can from his pocket. He took a long swallow and pointed at me, sputtering angrily, "You, you—"

He sat down hard on the wet sand, unable to finish his thought. "Lemme sleep," he said and lay down, closing his eyes. He didn't even flinch as cold waves splashed against his face, soaking his hair and leaving a trail of foam across his chin. The tide was rushing in. Within minutes it would rise to cover his face and drown him. *He won't be able to hurt my sister!*

Problem solved.

So simple.

Yet I could not walk away. If I let him die, I would be a murderer. And as much as I hated Ben, I was *not* a murderer. There had to be another way to save my sister.

I strained my back dragging him to safety. I left him facedown, behind a log on dry sand where the water would not reach him.

I stood and stretched and recognized the land where Suki's house sat in the year 2070. The hollowed-out space in the bank—where the Grady house would one day fit so snugly—was covered with sweet peas, the same purple wildflowers I had picked for the vase on our kitchen table.

It was a shock seeing Suki's house gone. I could not get used to the idea I'd actually traveled back in time. Yet I *had*. And I hastily reminded myself of the reason.

The sun had set, and the cliffs above cast cold, black shadows as I tucked my sunglasses into my back pocket and hurried back toward the party. I would find Rita and warn her! Of course, it wouldn't be that easy. I slowed down to ponder what I would say to her. I couldn't very well march up and announce, "I'm your sister who was born a hundred years in the future. I've traveled back in time to warn you your boyfriend is going to kill you."

She'd think I had brain-drag. There had to be another way to break them up.

Lost in thought, I rounded the corner. My mouth fell open as a figure came charging at me, her long brown hair flying wildly around her face.

Rita!

"Hey, chick! Where's Ben?" she demanded, her breath reeking of beer.

The moment was so familiar, I felt I'd lived it before. Suddenly I knew why. I'd read about it in her diary.

Was *I* the blonde she'd written about?

No! It's impossible! My mind whirled. *I couldn't have been here before.*

"Where's Ben?" Rita shouted.

"What's it to you?" I said. It was as if I were speaking the lines in a script. The words spilled from me, exactly as she had described in her diary.

I ducked my head, hiding my face, not ready for her to recognize me. She grabbed my arm. Her fingers dug painfully into my flesh.

No! She doesn't understand. She thinks I'm trying to hurt her. But it is Ben who will hurt her.

How could I make her understand? "Ben doesn't care about you!" I cried.

The word floated between us.

A warning.

From sister to sister.

Rita did not interpret it that way. Her hand came up, full force against my cheek. It was a cracking blow. I reeled, my head spinning, too shocked to speak.

A circle of teenagers closed in on us. The guys jeered, urging Rita to smack me again. The girls squealed and whispered to each other. I turned and bolted toward the bushes, scrambling for a place to hide from the curious stares. Then it hit me.

This was not the past. This was the *future*. My future! It might be 1970, but the plot unfolding was new to *me*. In Rita's diary the blonde ran for the bushes and was never seen again.

But that blonde wasn't just any blonde. It was me in my wig. I had just unwittingly reenacted a scene from Rita's diary so perfectly there could be no mistake. I had been here before. This was my past. Yet it was also my future. And my fate was in those bushes!

I skidded to a stop and stared into the dark, brambly

bushes clinging to the bank. My heart pounded. If I went in there now, did it mean no one would ever see me again?

Rita had written in her diary that "Tight Sweater" disappeared. She figured the blonde had gone back to where she'd come from. But I knew it couldn't be.

Something must have happened to me last time I was here. I wouldn't have gotten back in my time machine with my tail between my legs and headed for home. I'd *never* give up so easily. I was here to save my sister, and a slap on the face was not going to stop me. *What had stopped me before?*

An icy prickle of fear crept up my neck. Something far more sinister than a slap had prevented me from saving Rita.

Maybe I was *murdered* too. Perhaps Ben hadn't really passed out. Maybe he had followed me, waiting for an opportunity to attack.

Was he lurking in the bushes now?

I'd botched things last time. I wasn't going to mess up again. My sister's life—and perhaps my own—depended on my strategy. I darted away from the bank, raced through the crowd, and headed to the water's edge.

Cold waves lapped at my feet, soaking my tennis shoes.

There! I'd done it. I did not hide in the bushes as Rita had written in her diary.

A wonderful feeling of power rushed through me like a current of electricity. *I* was in charge of my destiny. Things did not have to fall into place exactly as they had before.

I had been here only forty minutes, and I'd already changed the past.

17

"ARE YOU OKAY?" SOMEONE ASKED, AND I GLANCED up at the most beautiful face I'd ever seen.

I'd been standing by the water's edge nearly ten minutes, wondering what to do next. It was dark now and the party was over. A round white moon peeked over Windy Cliff, lighting the face of the gorgeous guy who'd popped up beside me. "I'm Shane," he said, his full, sexy lips curving into an irresistible smile.

Mesmerized, I took in his liquid brown eyes, strong dimpled jaw, and lion's mane hair—wild gold locks spilling over wide shoulders.

"Shane Murdock!" I cried. *Ben's best friend!*

"You've heard of me?" he said, laughing. "Whatever you've heard, it isn't true."

He was right! Rita had written that he wasn't as attractive as Ben. For sisters, we certainly had different taste in boys!

Shane was short, perhaps an inch or two taller than my 5'6" height. He was solidly built and his tight T-shirt emphasized his muscular chest. My gaze swept his body, over faded jeans hugging narrow hips and down to his bare feet.

"Rita slugged you pretty hard," he said. "I guess she's jealous of you and Ben."

"She doesn't need to be," I said quickly. "I'm not interested in him."

"Rita's not used to drinking. She's usually pretty mellow."

"Did you see which way she went?" I asked.

"She left with April. Went home, I guess."

"Good." She was probably throwing up in her front yard right about now. In a minute, our mother would come outside, catch her, and put her on restrictions.

"So what happened to Ben?" Shane asked.

"He passed out."

He shook his head in amusement. "That sounds like Ben. I better make sure he's okay. Want to show me where he is?"

I was here for only one reason—to save my sister. Yet a walk in the moonlight with Shane sounded very appealing.

I hesitated, ashamed. My sister's life was at stake. How could I be so easily distracted?

But this was *research*. Shane could, after all, tell me something important about Rita and Ben that could help me break them up. I gestured toward the strip of land curving out to the sea and said, "Ben's way down there around the bend."

"I'm always dragging him home from somewhere," said Shane, falling into step beside me. "It keeps me in shape."

The tide was nearly in now, and the beach was just a thin stretch of rocky shore littered with logs and dried-out seaweed.

"Don't the barnacles hurt your feet?" I asked.

"I go barefoot so often the soles of my feet are like leather."

Agile as a cat, Shane moved along the beach, lightly leaping over the logs that blocked our path. I scrambled along behind him, and when we reached a particularly large log, he knelt on the top and offered his hand. The instant his flesh brushed mine, it was electrical. A current of excitement shot through me as his strong fingers closed over mine and he pulled me up onto the log. I lost my footing and teetered, nearly falling. But he firmly gripped my arms, steadying me as our eyes locked.

Our faces were inches apart, and as he gazed intently into my eyes, my heart thumped crazily. He said, "If I let you go, do you promise not to fall?"

I nodded and he released me from his gentle grasp and climbed down the other side of the log. As I followed, I felt a sudden breeze on my neck. I glanced up. My wig was snagged in a branch, dangling above me!

Shane regarded me with a grin and said, "Much better!"

Embarrassed, I snatched the wig from the branch. "I don't usually wear a wig."

"You shouldn't," he said softly. "You have beautiful hair,"

"So do you!" I'd never seen a guy with so much hair before. In my era, men wore their hair cropped close. Shane's hair shimmered sensuously in the moonlight. It was wild and free, and my fingers itched to dance through it.

"You look like your sister," he said, "only you're prettier than Rita."

"How did you know she's my sister?"

"It's obvious. Why haven't I met you before?"

"I've been away."

"Now that you're back, are you going to stay?" he asked the question casually, but his voice held a note of interest that made my heart skip. He wanted me to stay!

"It depends on how things go," I said and quickly changed the subject, asking him questions about himself. He told me he lived a mile from the beach and walked down here every night to watch the sunset, that he loved nature and wanted to live on a farm someday.

"I don't want to end up in a rut like my father and live in a plastic world with plastic people and clocks telling me what to do," he said, a hint of desperation leaking into his voice. "I want to get my hands in the dirt and watch green things grow and wake up with the sun."

The boys in 2070 never dreamed of becoming

farmers. Shane was like no boy I'd ever met. And I was touched he'd confided in me. I loved listening to the warm flow of his words and wished I could sail away on the sound of his voice.

"Is Ben around here somewhere?" he suddenly asked.

I'd forgotten about Ben. I'd forgotten *everything* except Shane.

"Oh!" I exclaimed. "I think we walked right past him."

After we'd backtracked fifty yards or so, I pointed to the log where I'd left Ben.

Shane looked behind it. "He's gone."

Gone? A chill blew through me. "But he passed out, how could he have—"

"Maybe one of the guys found him and helped him home," he said, shrugging. "Or maybe he woke up."

Or maybe he was slinking through the shadows, watching us!

We sat on the log, listening to the tide crawl in, its foamy fingers gently drumming the shore.

Brilliant moonlight washed over us, polishing everything so the sand glittered like silver and our skin seemed to glow from within. It was so incredibly bright I could clearly see the string of debris the waves had washed in—the long snake-like ropes of seaweed we called sea whips (mingled with the other stuff that resembled cooked spinach), shattered bits of clam shells, and various sized pieces of driftwood.

"Look," I said, pointing to a small, swirly white shell nestled in the seaweed by our feet.

"No one's home," said Shane, holding the shell between his fingers and peering into the opening. "Hermit crabs sometimes use these empty shells for houses."

"It's so pretty! I've never seen a shell like that."

"It's a frilled dogwinkle," he said. "They're all over."

Not in 2070! Had the animals who grew the lovely little shells become extinct?

I felt a wave of sadness for all the things that no longer existed in 2070. The homes of most of Rita's neighbors were gone—such as the house of the young mother I'd watched just hours before, so lovingly painting her shutters as her baby played nearby. Her home was probably bulldozed over by monstrous yellow machines with no respect for the memories it held. And I'd noticed a magnificent chestnut tree on the edge of Rita's yard that had disappeared by my time.

And what of the *people*—all the people, home in their beds this very moment? My real family, and the men, women, and kids who were *meant* to be my friends and neighbors? In the five minutes it would take me to travel a century, most of them would be long gone!

This handsome boy by my side would likely be dead when I returned to 2070.

But what if I *didn't* go back? What if I let my life unfold as it should have before science interfered? Things would still change, people would still die, but it would happen slowly. One loss at a time.

"Well, it doesn't look like Ben's going to show up," Shane said and pulled me to my feet.

The tide had crept in so far that we'd only made it halfway back when it became impossible to travel along the shore without icy waves slapping our feet, threatening to drench us.

Shane said, "There's a trail through the woods that leads to the road. Let's go that way and I'll walk you home."

Of course, I couldn't go home. My family didn't know I existed. But Shane wasn't aware of that, so I followed him up the sandy path. He knew his way through the brush and pointed out landmarks. "If you come this way again, turn left on the path before you get to the tree house," he instructed. "There's nothing but acres of blackberry bushes past it."

I wanted to see the tree house, so we strayed from the path to inspect the boxy wooden structure cradled in the maple's strong branches. "Who does it belong to?"

"Probably some kid," said Shane. "I discovered it one day when it started pouring. I waited out the storm in there."

It wasn't anything fancy, but it was shelter. I knew where I would sleep.

Shane walked me all the way to Banbury House. I strolled up the walk to the front porch, as if planning to go inside. I waved to Shane, and when he rounded the corner, I backtracked, staying in the shadows by the side of the road—just in case Ben was lurking around!

Safely nestled in the house in the tree, I gazed out at Puget Sound, inky black below the bright moon. The tree house was pieced together with odd scraps of wood and not much bigger than a closet. I sat down on a sleeping bag I found curled up in the corner and inhaled the sweet spring air, my mind spinning. There had already been so much to think about. And now there was Shane.

Shane. I said it out loud. "Shane!" I loved the taste of his name on my tongue.

Was I being disloyal to Kyle?

It wasn't as if Kyle and I were getting married. For all I knew, I might never see Kyle again. Even if I decided to return to 2070, I might not be capable of it.

Now that I was back where I belonged, I could stay forever. The idea appealed to me. But it brought with it a hot rush of guilt. How could I so easily abandon my 2070 life? Was my mother worrying about me?

I didn't want to think about that! That woman wasn't even my real mother. She was simply the person who had lied to me for seventeen years. A fresh surge of anger burst through me, strengthening my resolve.

As for Kyle . . .

Yes, I still cared for him. But something happened to me when I was near Shane. No boy had ever made me feel that way before. I closed my eyes, relishing the hug he had given me when he left me at Banbury House. As our bodies pressed together, it felt as if our souls touched.

I fell asleep, imagining Shane's strong arms still around me. And—amazingly—I slept through the night, not waking until the morning sun stained the distant mountains pink. But it was not the light that woke me. It was fear. For the first thing I heard the next morning was an angry voice whispering. "Don't move or I'll blow your head off."

MY EYES POPPED OPEN AND I STIFLED A SCREAM. The short, black gun was inches from my face, aimed between my eyes.

"Don't shoot!" I cried.

A grubby finger pulled the trigger and a stream of water splashed my forehead. It was only a squirt gun!

A little boy with a mop of blond hair glared at me. "Who said you could sleep in my tree house?" he demanded.

"I'm sorry," I said, wiping the water from my face with my sleeve. "I didn't have any anyplace else to sleep."

"I don't allow girls in here," he informed me. "You better not have gotten into my stuff!"

He was somehow familiar. I studied his impish, freckled face and asked, "What's your name?"

"I'm Chuck, and my brother built this house for me, so get out."

Of course! I'd read about Chuck, Rita's pesky neighbor, in her diary. Yet the familiarity went beyond that. Why did I feel as if I knew him?

"Look, Chuck, I'm really sorry. But I didn't get into your things. I'll leave if you really want me to."

His squinty green eyes darted about suspiciously, finally resting on a wooden box in the corner. He moved to sit beside it, guarding its contents.

"What's in there?" I asked. "Your comic book collection?"

"None of your business."

"Do you know where the high school is?" I asked. "Did you see your neighbor Rita leave for school this morning?"

"You sure ask a lot of questions," he said defensively.

I tried another tactic. "You know, Chuck, this is the frazzinest tree house I've ever seen!"

"What's 'frazzinest' mean?" he asked.

"When something's frazzin, it means it's really great," I explained. "Like the best."

"It *is* a great tree house," he said, beaming proudly.

"Your brother must have worked really hard to build it for you."

"Yeah!" he said, his eyes shining with a memory. "And I helped him."

"You did? You must be some frazzin carpenter."

"I pounded lots of the nails in all by myself," he said, leaning back on his elbows. Soon he was answering my questions. I learned that it was now almost nine and that the high school classes had already started. Chuck drew me a map, and I was surprised to see Rita's school was located in the same spot as mine.

"It was nice to meet you, Chuck," I said and stuck out my hand to shake.

He jerked away. "I don't shake hands with girls," he said, apologetically. "They have cooties."

For a second, he looked almost sad to see me go, and my heart twisted in sympathy as I remembered what Rita had written about his home life. But there was no time to think about it. I needed to find my sister!

By the time I'd walked to the high school, the first class had let out and the hallways were jammed with people.

"Do you know Rita Mills?" I asked a tall girl in a plaid skirt who was shoving books into a locker.

"I've heard her name," she said, eyeing me strangely. "But I don't know her."

Why was she looking at me like that? Why was *everyone* staring at me?

Though I'd slept in my clothes, my jeans weren't that wrinkled. But every place I turned, kids were pointing and gawking. I couldn't figure it out until a teacher confronted me.

"What are you trying to prove, coming to school dressed like that?" he demanded, his frog eyes glaring from behind thick glasses. "If you want to look like a boy after school, that's your business. But when you set foot in this school you are to look and behave like a young lady. If you do not follow the dress code, you will be expelled."

Glancing around, I realized that all the other girls wore skirts or dresses.

A group of girls walked by and clapped. "Right on!" one yelled and flashed me the peace sign.

"What's your name?" the teacher asked, his whiny voice sharpening with annoyance. "I can't believe your homeroom teacher didn't send you to the principal. Go see him now! I know Mr. Pratt will tell you to go home and change into a skirt."

"I don't have a skirt," I admitted.

"Do not smart-mouth me, miss!" he snapped.

"Sorry," I mumbled and found the closest exit and left the school, shaking my head. I couldn't believe it. Girls not allowed to wear pants!

Across the street I ordered a cup of water at a fast-food restaurant and sat on the curb, listening to my stomach grumble and wishing I had money for food.

When the sun was high in the bright blue sky, the school's big red doors flung open and kids poured out. Lunchtime. A herd of teenagers stampeded toward the restaurant.

I studied the noisy crowd. Giggling girls, shouting boys. If I just looked at the faces, it was no different than watching the swarm of students that populated my high school. But as my eyes traveled over the clothing and hairstyles, I was once again struck by the fact that this was no longer 2070.

The girls in Rita's school wore short bright-colored

skirts with tucked-in blouses, knee socks, and saddle shoes. The boys wore colorful bell-bottom pants. Their shirts were made from slippery-looking fabric with loud designs and sported ridiculously large collars. The kids from my era would laugh if they could see these styles.

It was all perspective, of course. The styles of 2070 would look ludicrous to these kids. But these were the styles I was meant to wear. And these were the kids that should have been my peers. *If* I'd been born when I should have been.

Was it possible to fit in now? Had I stepped back in time to claim my rightful place? Was there any way the Mills family—my family—could grasp the fact that I'd traveled through time to be with them? Would they love and accept me?

Though I'd come here to save Rita, in the back of my mind, I'd longed to be here for *me*. My life in 2070 was nothing more than a lie. It was unnatural. But this was *real*. This was my time.

"It's not fair Mr. Frink made you leave."

Startled, I glanced up to see a petite, pretty girl in a red dress smiling at me. She shuffled an armload of books and tossed her head so her long amber hair sailed over her shoulder. "We're tired of being forced to wear skirts to school," she said, gesturing to the group of girls beside her.

"It's not right," I agreed.

"Yeah," chimed in a busty girl in pigtails with round brown glasses. "The boys are allowed to be comfortable. Can you imagine if *they* were forced to wear dresses?"

"Why should we have to show off our legs for the boys?" asked a girl with cinnamon skin whose hair was bubbled up into an Afro.

"I think it's pretty stupid too," I said.

"My cousin at Foster High School organized a protest," she added. "Nine senior girls came to school in jeans."

"What happened?" I asked.

"They were sent home and suspended for three days. But if enough of us get together we could make a change."

"Right on!" The blond-haired girl said, and pumped her fist in the air. "Women's Lib is here to stay!"

My vow to remain inconspicuous withered up and blew away on the breeze as I found myself in the middle of a protest.

In the restaurant, a half dozen girls squeezed into the orange vinyl booth beside me, sharing limp, salty french fries and discussing the protest.

"It's so cool you started this protest," Pam, the pig-tailed girl, told me. I grinned back at her, feeling oddly at ease with these strangers. Teresa, Celia, Lynn, Pam, Laura, Becky. They would have been my friends—*if only I'd been born when I was meant to be!*

I was soon caught up in the excitement of the dress code rebellion as we giggled and joked. I felt charged with the energy at that table as we made plans and talked about the awful Mr. Frink.

"You know," Lynn said, "you sure look like Rita Mills. Are you guys related?"

Without thinking, I nodded. "Yes, she's my sister."

Perhaps it wasn't the smartest thing to tell people I was Rita's sister, when she herself did not know I existed. But it was the truth, and it just popped out.

My new friends accepted the fact, and I was relieved when they didn't question me. I sat facing the window and scanned the parking lot, searching for any sign of my sister.

I did not know how I would warn her about Ben—only that I had to do it soon. But I'm ashamed to admit that I momentarily forgot Rita as I listened to the girls discuss "Women's Lib." It was fascinating to learn that in 1970, women were usually the secretaries and nurses, while the men were the executives and doctors. In 2070, women's accomplishments not only equaled men's, they actually surpassed them somewhat!

"Someday, *women* will run the country," I volunteered.

"Right on!" Lynn yelled, and I smiled at her enthusiasm. I wished I could tell her that all the presidents in my lifetime had been women.

We'd studied Women's Liberation in history class, but at the time it had seemed like an ancient topic that had nothing to do with my life. Now, listening to this group of girls who felt so oppressed, I was inspired by the fire in their eyes, their resolve to make things right.

Swept away by the excitement, it caught me completely off guard when someone tapped my shoulder. I turned to see a familiar girl, her cheeks flushed pink, her hazel eyes blazing.

Rita!

"Why are you telling everyone you're my sister?" she demanded. Her anger gave way to shock as she stared at me.

"I can explain," I said. "Let's go outside."

I rushed ahead of her—out the double doors, across the paved parking lot—not ready to look her in the eye.

What would I say to her? How could she possibly believe I had traveled from the future? *I* could hardly believe it myself.

"Let's sit here," I said and settled on a short brick wall bordering a flower bed where tall red geraniums bobbed their heads in the breeze.

"I don't want to sit!" Rita cried, her eyes round with astonishment, her hands clenched into fists at her sides. "*Who* are you?"

As I stared back at her confused face, I wanted to leap up and throw my arms around her—to hug her close and keep her safe forever. My sister was *alive*! And I was actually there with her. The enormity of that fact sent a crushing wave of emotion through me and I blinked away tears.

The truth was so incredible—so *unbelievable*—I decided to give her just half of it. I said, "Did you know your parents made an embryo for Twin-Star Labs?"

"How did *you* know that?" she asked. "What does that have to do with you?"

"That embryo was put inside a surrogate mother in Idaho," I said, forcing myself to speak calmly. "I am the result."

"That's not possible!" she whispered. "The embryo is still in the freezer at Twin-Star. I've seen the container myself."

I thought fast. "The containers holding the embryos were mismarked," I said, the lie flying from my lips. "I was implanted inside my mother almost immediately after my conception seventeen years ago."

Rita gasped, her face slack with shock.

"*Look at me!*" I cried. "Can't you see we're sisters?"

"Yes," she said slowly. "I guess I can." Her knees seemed to fold involuntarily as she sank down beside me. She could not peel her eyes from my face, an almost mirror image hers.

"My name is Jenna. I came here for a reason. I have something very important to tell you."

She squeezed my hand, her fingers icy. "I always wanted a sister," she said breathlessly. "I can't believe this is happening."

"I know. I was shocked to find out about you too. I only learned the truth a little while ago. I spent my whole life thinking the woman who raised me was my real mother."

"Do our parents know you're here?"

"They think I'm still a frozen embryo. I'm not ready for them to know about me. So much has happened so fast. And the truth is, I came here to see you. Will you please try to be open-minded about what I have to tell you?"

She laughed nervously. "Is it something awful? You look scared."

"I *am* scared," I admitted. I took a deep breath. "The thing is, I'm psychic—*very* psychic. I came here because I'm worried about you. I saw something in your future, Rita. Something terrible!"

"What did you see?"

Before I could respond, someone moved up beside her and threw his arms around her shoulders. Her eyes lit with pleasure and she kissed him on the cheek. It was Ben.

19

I WORRIED BEN WOULD REMEMBER ME FROM THE night before. But his eyes held no glimmer of recognition—only amazed curiosity. He looked from me to Rita and back again, obviously struck by our resemblance.

"You're not going to believe this, Ben," Rita said. "This is my sister."

"I didn't know you had a sister. What a trip!"

I regarded him coolly and said, "Yes, it is kind of a vacation."

Rita smiled. "He means a mind trip. Don't they use that expression in Iowa?"

"*Idaho,*" I corrected her. "I'm from Idaho."

"Far out," Ben said.

"Well, it's not *that* far out," I said. "Just one state away."

"I think she's putting us on," Rita said.

"Right on!" I said, grabbing for one of the new expressions I'd learned. It wasn't easy getting used to the odd phrases kids in 1970 used. Rita had used some of these expressions in her diary, but they still echoed strangely in my ear. I forced myself to laugh, so they'd believe I *was* just putting them on.

Ben laughed too, his blue eyes sparkling. *So this is what a killer looks like when he's sober,* I thought bitterly. He seemed taller than last night. Probably because he was standing straighter.

I was sure now Ben didn't recognize me. He probably didn't even remember the evening. Was he so drunk he blacked the whole thing out?

Ben sat down and slid his arm around Rita's waist. Smiling contentedly, she rested her head on his shoulder.

Startled, I realized that when Rita wrote about this day, she and Ben had not yet made up. Obviously things were unfolding much differently than they had in the diary. My presence here had already made an impact.

"Why didn't you tell me you had a sister?" Ben asked Rita.

"*I* didn't know," she replied. "And I can't possibly concentrate on school today so I'm skipping the rest of my classes. Ben, it's going to blow your mind when you hear where Jenna came from. It's a really weird story—"

"It's a *long* story," I cut her off. "And Rita and I

have lots of catching up to do." I stood and grabbed her hand, tugging her away from Ben.

His eyes widened in annoyed surprise as I pulled Rita from his arms. Thrown off balance, she fell against me. "Let's walk home," I said, still clinging to her hand.

She giggled nervously and held her other hand out to Ben. Her slim white fingers were lost as his big hand folded over hers. "Ben can give us a ride," she said.

I did not want to let go of her, and neither did he. It was like we were playing an odd game of tug-of-war with Rita as the prize. My eyes met Ben's. I glared coldly. He stared back with an icy challenge of his own.

"Quit pulling on me, you guys!" Rita laughed, oblivious to the hostile exchange between us.

Ben drove us home in his '59 Chevy—a rounded, dusty, sputtering vehicle that lurched forward with each stop. As I bounced about in the backseat, watching Rita watching Ben, doubt crept over me. She was cuddled up to him and her eyes shined so adoringly when she gazed at him. How would I keep her away from him? How would I tell my sister the truth about the boy she loved?

"It looks like my parents aren't home," Rita announced as Ben pulled into the driveway of Banbury House. I felt both relief and disappointment. I wanted so much to see my real parents. Of course, I could not meet them—not unless I was prepared to tell them the truth. Rita had believed my lie about the embryos getting mixed up. But our parents would surely look into matters.

We got out of the car, and Rita leaned through the window and passionately kissed her boyfriend good-bye.

"Want to walk on the beach?" she asked me as Ben's car chugged away and disappeared around the corner. "It's such a gorgeous day, we can hang out there until the sun sets."

"I thought you were grounded," I said.

"Not me! Why do you say that?"

"I heard you got pretty drunk last night. I figured you'd be in trouble."

"I *would* have been! But Mom didn't catch me. She and Dad went out for Chinese food and ran into some friends. They got home after I did."

According to Rita's diary, our mother had found her throwing up in the yard and grounded her. Why had things unfolded so differently this time?

"I can thank Tiny Tim for saving my butt," Rita said.

"Who?"

"Tiny Tim. He's my cat. He jumped up on the counter and ate a big chunk out of the tuna casserole Mom made for dinner. That's why my parents decided to go out to eat."

So that was it! I'd let the cat out of the attic. Last time around, he must have been shut in the attic, unable to get to the casserole.

Rita gave me a tour of Banbury House. The wood floors that Mom was so proud of did not shine in Rita's time. Dulled by dust and a big family's footsteps, they were covered in places by the same type of shaggy carpet Rita had in her room.

In the living room a long vinyl couch, flanked by end tables with voluptuous green lamps, faced a noisy black-and-white television. "My kid brother must have gotten home early because of the parent-teacher conference," Rita said, turning off the TV. "He always turns the TV on full blast and then runs outside to play."

Olive-green, vivid oranges, and earthy brown seemed to be the color scheme for 1970 decorating. It was as if Banbury House was dressed for a costume party in funky clothes. If I had traveled back in time *two* centuries, I would probably have found more familiar decor, because Mom had very carefully decorated in authentic Victorian.

The Mills family decorating made more sense. Why try to imitate a thing of the past? People should live in the time and place they were *meant* to. As I watched my smiling sister, I knew I was meant to be *here*.

"It's beautiful," I said, gazing out the bay window at the sweeping view of Puget Sound's glittering blue water. I pretended to see it for the first time. "You're lucky."

"It's really blowing my mind that I suddenly have a sister," Rita said. "But I'm glad you found me, Jenna."

"Ever since I learned about you, I could hardly think of anything else," I admitted.

Meeting my sister was as wonderful as I'd imagined. It was as if I'd found my other half. Looking into Rita's eyes was like passing through a doorway into a familiar place where I was welcome and comfortable.

There was none of the self-consciousness that usually goes with meeting someone new. We understood each other so well it was scary.

Rita loved the sound of wind chimes tinkling in the breeze. "It sounds like mermaids laughing," she said, tilting her head and listening to the faint jingling of faraway chimes as we headed for the beach.

"Maybe it is," I said. I could imagine the milky-skinned creatures bobbing to the surface, their huge green eyes blinking away bits of seaweed as their sweet peals of laughter drifted away on the wind.

"My friend April thinks I'm crazy when I say stuff like that," Rita said. "But you understand."

"We think alike. We're *sisters*."

Rita and I both loved the feel of the salty breeze combing through our hair, the color blue, and raw chocolate chip cookie dough. We were both allergic to bees, had fierce tempers, and rebelled against authority.

I had known, of course, that we were alike. I'd sensed that from her diary. In the flesh, it was more apparent. Strolling together along the beach, our strides matched step for step. And we stared at each other in amazement as we continually opened our mouths in the same instant to say the same thing.

But there was one difference I didn't want to think about. *Ben*.

She loved him. I hated him.

"What were you going to tell me earlier?" Rita asked as we rested on a log, watching sand fleas leap around our bare feet.

I picked up a stick and drew a lazy circle in the gray sand. How could I tell her *here*? Ben had killed her on the beach, probably near this spot.

"It's hard to talk about," I told her. "I'll tell you later."

Later came much too soon. The sun set—another fiery display of brilliant red shades. "Strawberry pop," I said, remembering how she'd described such a sunset in her diary.

"That's what I was thinking!" She stretched her arms up and tipped her head back as if to drink in the sky and gleefully shouted, "The sky looks like strawberry pop!"

As we headed up the path to Banbury House, she promised to hide me in her room, where she assured me our parents rarely ventured. "They know I don't like them invading my space," she explained.

Rita ran around the house, peering through windows until she spotted our parents sitting in the dining room. She brought me through the front and we slipped up the stairs to her room as our mother called, "Rita, is that you?"

My heart lurched at the sound of her voice. It was rich and silky and seemed to wrap around me as I froze on the staircase. *Mother!*

My legs suddenly felt as soft and limp as worn-out feather pillows and I imagined myself collapsing—tumbling down the stairs into a heap where my mother would find me and be sorry for deserting me.

"Yes!" Rita called. "What do you want?"

"The Daisy Garden Gift Shop might sell some of my pottery on consignment. Did they call while I was out?"

"How should I know?" Rita said loudly, rolling her eyes for my benefit. "I haven't even been home!"

She nudged me and we hurried up to her room, where we talked until our voices were hoarse.

I was surprised when no one called Rita down for dinner. "We're informal around here," she explained. "I became a vegetarian last year, and Mom's given up trying to make me eat her weird meaty casseroles. Mostly we just scrounge what we can find."

"I'm a vegetarian too," I said. "Where I come from, everybody is!"

"Far out," she said and went to make us sandwiches.

When we got ready for bed, Rita flicked off the lights and held a match to a fat colorful candle poking from a pop bottle on her dresser. "It's a strobe candle," she told me. "Some of my posters are blacklight posters and they look really cool in this light."

The candle's tall flame flickered wildly. In the eerie, jerking light, the images in the posters seemed to leap and dance.

We sat on opposite ends of the lumpy green sleeping bag that Rita had rolled out for me beside her bed.

"Crystal Blue Persuasion" played on the record player. I remembered the first time I'd heard it. It reminded me of the blue rays that had brought me here to Rita—crystal blue rays shooting from my visor.

"What are you thinking now?" Rita asked, her eyes staring eagerly into mine.

"I'm just listening to the song," I fibbed, wishing I could tell her the truth. We'd shared so much in the last hours. I'd told her all about the people back home. The parents who raised me. My strange neighbor, Suki. My boyfriend, Kyle. I just didn't mention that none of these people existed yet.

By now, Rita knew I wanted to be an artist, was terrified of speaking in front of groups, and had once fallen from a window and broken my arm.

I knew Rita had wet her pants in the middle of a second grade math test (it was the teacher's fault because she wouldn't let her go to the rest room), cried for three days when her hamster died, and had stolen a candy bar from the corner grocery store when she was ten. Still feeling guilty, three years later, she'd anonymously mailed them a dime to pay for it.

"I want us to know *everything* about each other," Rita said.

If I told her *everything,* would she believe me?

For now, it was enough to be with her—to hear her secrets, to hear her laugh. From the moment I first heard Rita laugh, I felt whole. She had one of those laughs that fly right out and fill a room. Fat and warm, it came straight from the bottom of her belly and bounced off the furniture.

Most of the girls I'd known had high-pitched giggles that flattened self-consciously as soon as they hit a sour note.

Not Rita. She let laughter leap from her in great unselfconscious bounds.

When she laughed, her mouth opened wide, revealing two pointy little teeth in the top row of her mouth. They looked like fangs. That night in her room, the light from the strobe candle glinted on them as her head bobbed about.

When Rita laughed, I couldn't help but laugh with her. The sound of us laughing together made me happy. Our voices meshed together, harmonious as a symphony.

We were having such a good time, I hated to broach an ugly subject. Yet I *had* to warn her. It was, after all, what I had come for.

"I wish I didn't have to tell you this," I began. "But I can't put it off any longer."

She sat cross-legged, facing me. She was still smiling and I couldn't bear to wipe the happy sparkle from her eyes.

"Go on," she urged.

I drew a long breath and plunged ahead. "I had a premonition. It was bad. *Really* bad. It was about Ben."

"Ben!" she whispered, her eyes widening in alarm. "You think something is going to happen to Ben?"

"He's going to hurt you."

"He's going to break my heart?" Her voice shrunk with worry. "You think he's going to dump me?"

"I wish it was that. But it's worse. Oh, Rita! He's going to *really* hurt you. He's going to beat you."

It took a moment for my words to register on her face. Her eyes flickered between confusion, shock, and then amusement. "That's ridiculous!" she scoffed. "Ben wouldn't hurt a fly! And he certainly wouldn't hurt *me*!"

"In my vision," I continued, my voice wavering, "Ben killed you."

"You're *wrong*!" she snapped, anger crawling into her voice.

"I'm very psychic," I said.

"Psychics make mistakes," she said brusquely. "I'm psychic too, and I know Ben would never hurt me. He *loves* me."

"If he does, it's a sick love. A twisted, warped love! If you don't stay away from him, he'll beat you to *death*!"

"How can you say that?" Rita cried. "You don't even know Ben!"

"I know a killer when I see one," I said quietly.

She flinched as if I'd slapped her.

I shouldn't have told her so much so soon. I shouldn't have told her so brutally.

But I didn't know of a nice way to tell someone her boyfriend was going to kill her.

She sat as still as a stick, staring at me, eyes huge and confused, lips pursed.

"Rita," I said helplessly and gently touched her arm. She jerked away and turned her back to me.

"Rita, please!"

"Drop it, Jenna," she said coldly. "It's late. Let's get some sleep."

She refused to hear another word about Ben.

Rita woke me the next morning with a bowl of granola. "Room service!" she said, tapping the spoon on the side of the porcelain bowl. I regarded her drowsily and inched from the sleeping bag. She was already dressed and her long hair gleamed in the soft morning light that floated through the window.

"I hope you like strawberries on your cereal. Mom got them from an organic greenhouse," said my smiling sister, apparently ready to forgive and forget last night.

If only it was that simple.

The night before we'd chosen our outfits for the dress code protest: faded blue jeans and flowing blouses. Rita loaned me a pink flowered blouse with puffed sleeves. She called it a "peasant shirt." She wore a blue blouse with polka dots. She lifted her hair to show me huge silver peace signs dangling from her ears.

"Far out," I said.

As she dug through her closet, searching for her moccasins, I sat at the dresser, brushing my hair. It was the same dresser I used in 2070, one of the few pieces of furniture that shared a history with Banbury House.

"Do you have any lip tinter?" I asked and opened the drawer. Sure enough, she kept her makeup in the same place I'd kept mine. Scanning Rita's assortment of tubes and compacts, I spotted a familiar item. "Oh!" I cried.

"What's wrong?" Rita asked, peering over my shoulder.

"Nothing," I said, trying to hide my confusion. "I just found my strawberry lip tinter. I don't remember putting it in there."

"That's weird-looking lipstick!" She said and snatched it from my hand.

My heart was pounding fast. I had not brought the lip tinter with me. Yet here it was! How did it get here?

Then I knew. *I* had sent it here. By accident. And I'd accused Suki of stealing it!

Before I'd even known about my PK abilities, I was crackling with psychic energy. Apparently—*without the aid of a visor*—I'd sent my lip tinter on a trip, just as Rita had sent her paper clip on one. I had inadvertently snatched Rita's paper clip from its journey, and she'd done the same to my lip tinter.

There was such an incredible connection between my sister and me that we were sending objects back and forth through time to each other *without even realizing it*! It was as if we knew one another before we'd heard of each other's existence.

"How do you put this lipstick on?" Rita asked. Her eyes were so clear and bright, her smile so trusting. It hurt to look at her—to know she was in danger.

"Let me show you," I said, blinking away tears.

"See, there's a tiny needle here and when you push this button it injects color into your lips."

"A *needle*? You're kidding!"

"It doesn't hurt," I assured her and jabbed my bottom lip. Within seconds, my lips deepened to a bright berry shade.

"*Far out!* I've never seen anything like that!"

"We're kind of ahead of our time in Idaho," I said. "The needle has a self-sterilizing mechanism, so you can use it too."

"How long will it last?" she asked as she injected her lips.

"About eight hours. It will fade by tonight," I said and crossed the room to roll up my sleeping bag. As I did so, something outside caught my eye. I moved to the window, just in time to see an arm disappearing into a shrub.

"Rita!" I cried. "He's out there! He's watching us!"

"Who?" she asked, crowding in beside me.

"Ben."

"*Ben?* Did you see him?"

"No," I admitted. "But it had to be him."

"Why would Ben creep around in the bushes? If he wanted to see me, he'd knock on our front door."

How could she understand? She didn't have the proof I did. She hadn't read of her murder in the newspaper.

Shuddering, I turned away and shoved my feet into the sneakers she'd loaned me. Unspoken words of warning scorched my mouth. I swallowed hard and clamped my lips together, not trusting myself to speak.

Rita was so sloopy in love with Ben, she would not hear anything bad about him. If I kept pushing, I feared she'd send me away.

How in the world would I protect her then?

20

AS WE HIKED UP THE HILL TO THE SCHOOL, WE made up a story about me to tell Rita's friends.

"Please don't tell them the truth," I'd begged her. "Everyone will think I'm a freak."

"Because you were conceived in a test tube?" she said. "I think it's kind of cool."

But she went along with my request and we thought of two good stories. The first was that I was her cousin and the second was that I was her sister who had been raised by an aunt. We hadn't yet decided on which lie to use when we reached the school, so we ended up telling both versions to different people.

As it turned out, no one paid much attention because they were so excited about the protest. "Hey, you guys!" Lynn yelled as we headed for Rita's locker. "Over here!"

We hurried over to the jean clad girls who were clustered in conspiracy at the end of the hall. "How many of us are there?" Rita asked.

"We've counted twenty-four!" Lynn said, beaming. "But Charlotte Wade and April Peters chickened out. Charlotte's wearing *culottes*! As if that counts!"

"Culottes are already allowed," Rita said. "Anyway, they look just like a skirt. But what's *April's* problem?"

"Her dad saw her leaving the house in her Levi's and threatened to ground her."

"Bummer," Rita said.

"Yeah," Lynn agreed. "My parents were home when I left the house, so I brought my jeans to school in a paper bag and changed in the girls' room.

"Hey," Lynn said, nudging me. "Look who's freaking out."

We followed her gaze across the hall to where Mr. Frink stood in the doorway, his frog eyes about popping out of his glasses as he stared at us.

Lynn flashed him the peace sign. She was at least a head shorter than everyone else, but tougher than any girl I'd ever met. "This is a revolution not a war!" she called out to Mr. Frink. His slippery lips parted as if he were about to speak, but no words came out. He looked so ridiculous that Rita started giggling and buried her face in my shoulder so he wouldn't see.

A moment later, he was bustling toward the office, the starched thighs of his slacks scratching against each other with each indignant step.

I jumped when the bell rang. "Come on," Rita said. "I've got to get to homeroom."

We sat in the back of the room and watched the students stream in. My heart sped when Shane appeared in the doorway. I followed his confident stride as he crossed to his desk. He swung a leg over the back of his chair and sat down. His hair spilled over the back of the chair, swinging sensuously each time he moved his head.

A thin girl in a short red skirt and a yellow knit vest plopped herself possessively on top of his desk. She leaned toward him flirtatiously, her square brown glasses sliding down her pointy nose.

"Who's that girl?" I asked Rita.

"That's my friend April. She's got the hots for Shane, but he doesn't dig her. He's too nice of a guy to tell her to get lost."

Was that why he'd treated me kindly? Because he was a nice guy? Had I only imagined the attraction between us?

Rita said, "I'm going to see if Shane knows where Ben is."

I wished I could go with her as she crossed the room to talk to Shane. But our moonlit walk now seemed like a dream and I was suddenly shy under the harsh lights of the classroom.

Rita whispered something to Shane and he looked up, caught me staring, and his face broke into a dimpled grin. Flustered, I turned away, pretending to be fascinated with the maps covering the wall behind me.

Rita returned to her seat just as Mrs. Vince entered.

She was a nervous little bird-like teacher with pursed lips and hair in a stiff bun. Her pinched face emptied of color as she spotted the five girls in jeans. Quickly and quietly, she began scribbling on a scrap of paper.

"She's writing down our names," Rita whispered knowingly. "I heard her ask someone who *you* are, so I guess you're going to get busted right along with the rest of us."

When Mrs. Vince hurried from the room, her pointy brown shoes clicking sharply across the tile floor, everyone started talking. "Mrs. Vince is freaked," Shane said, laughing. "She hasn't acted like this since the bomb threat."

"What's the big deal?" asked Rita. "Girls should be comfortable too!"

"Right on!" Shane said, gazing directly at me.

A moment later, the strained voice of Mr. Pratt, the principal, poured through the speaker on the wall as he read the names of the girls involved in the protest and barked, "Come to the office immediately."

There were 29 of us in all, too many to fit in the straight-backed chairs that lined one wall of the office. Some of the girls smiled smugly, but a couple nervously chewed on their lips. Rita kept pinching my arm, trying to keep herself from giggling. She got me going and I started laughing too.

"You think this is funny?" asked Mr. Pratt. He was a short, round man with angry blue eyes that swept disgustedly over our outfits. "This is a high school, not a hippie haven," he snapped.

Lynn said, "You can't have one set of rules for the

boys and another for the girls. If they can wear pants, then so should *we*! We'll get a lawyer if we need to."

"We'll see about that," he replied crisply and began writing down the phone numbers of parents.

When he realized I wasn't enrolled in the school, he asked for my parents' number anyway.

"They can't be reached at work," I said quickly.

"Young lady, I've had enough of your games—"

"She's telling the truth," Rita interrupted. "My parents are at work too, but if you call this number someone will pick us up." She wrote a number on a piece of paper and handed it to him.

As he scrutinized it, Rita assured him, "He's a responsible adult, Mr. Pratt. My parents trust him."

Mr. Pratt scurried into the other room and Rita whispered, "Sky will come get us. He's cool."

Half an hour later, a young man with fine shoulder-length blond hair pulled back into a ponytail strolled in, whistling a jaunty tune. He had the same emerald green eyes as Kyle.

"This is Sky Mettley," Rita told me.

Kyle's grandfather! My mouth fell open.

"Sky's the only one at Twin-Star I trust," said Rita.

"That's because I'm the only one there under thirty," he said, winking at me.

Mr. Pratt had stepped out, and his bubble-haired secretary eyed Sky suspiciously. Rita noticed and nudged him. Sky cleared his throat and said sternly, "I'm surprised at you girls. This isn't proper attire for young ladies."

We hurried out to the hallway and Rita burst into

giggles. "An Academy Award for you, Sky!" she said. "Let's get out of here before Mr. Pratt comes back."

"You and Rita sure look a lot alike," Sky said as he shoved open the double doors and we left the sterile, tiled halls of the school behind. "Are you related?"

Rita opened her mouth to reply, but her eyes met mine and I shook my head. "We're cousins," she said, blushing with the lie.

We climbed into Sky's pickup truck and he drove us to Twin-Star Labs—a decidedly more modest building than the Twin-Star of the twenty-first century.

As Rita showed me around the lab, Sky watched me quizzically. Something told me he did not believe we were cousins.

When he left us alone for a minute, I said, "He's sure young for a scientist."

"He's more like an *aspiring* scientist," Rita explained. "Sky is just an assistant."

"But he invented the visor!"

"How did you know he was working on a visor?" Rita asked with surprise. "That's a top secret project that hardly anybody knows about!"

"I told you I was psychic."

"Maybe, but you're off base on this one. Sky didn't invent the visor. Dr. Crowell did. He's this old bald dude who is a total bore. Sky was helping him with the visor and Dr. Crowell split right in the middle of the project. I think Sky's hoping he won't come back so he can take credit for it."

I couldn't believe it. Kyle was so proud of his

grandfather and now it turned out he hadn't even invented the visor! How could I tell Kyle? He'd be crushed!

I knew I couldn't hurt Kyle with the information, and vowed to keep the secret—*if* I returned to 2070.

"I think Sky likes you," Rita said. "Did you notice how he kept staring at you?"

I didn't think so. I had the oddest feeling he'd guessed who I was.

21

BEFORE THE MORNING WAS OVER, I FOUND MYSELF agreeing with Rita's assessment of the gentle soft-spoken scientist. If "cool" meant the same as "frazzin," then Sky was *definitely* "cool."

Maybe it was because he was young, but Sky seemed so different from the scientists I knew— stodgy old men who didn't know how to have fun.

Sky took us to lunch at the hangout across the street from the school and as I watched him joking with Rita, I wondered if I dared tell him how I came to be there.

What if he didn't approve of the fact I'd stolen the visor? I had, after all, committed a crime. If the wrong people found out, who knew what would happen to me!

When Rita went to the rest room, Sky pointedly asked me to tell him about myself.

"Not much to tell," I said.

"You and Rita sure look alike—even for cousins." His gaze was steady on my face. "Are you related to her dad's or mom's side?"

I stared at my french fries, wondering if I looked more like my biological mother or father.

Rita returned and saved me from answering because she had a question of her own. "Will you do us a favor, Sky? Ben wants to have a kegger on the beach tonight and we need someone to buy the beer."

"I've only been twenty-one for six months, and I've just about worn out my I.D. buying beer for your friends," he said with a grin. "Besides, I don't have time to party. I've got to get back to work on my project."

"*Your* project?" Rita said, laughing. "Two weeks ago you were making coffee for Dr. Crowell, and now you're in charge. Next thing you know, you'll be taking credit for the whole thing!"

A deep flush crept up Sky's neck, and his eyes lowered with embarrassment. Rita had hit a sensitive nerve. Obviously he was a proud man, just like Kyle, who got the same look on his face when the kids needled him about his wealth.

The memory of Kyle tugged at my heart. Would I ever see him again? What if things didn't work out here and I decided to travel back to 2070 only to find I *couldn't*?

"Don't turn into a square like Dr. Crowell," Rita

teased Sky. "Just because you're sitting at his desk now."

"Okay, okay!" He said, shaking his head good-naturedly. "I'll pick up the keg *this* time. But find another sucker next time."

After Sky drove us home, I nervously asked Rita, "Do we have to go to the party?"

Though I hadn't mentioned it again, she knew I was worried about her. "Would you please stop being paranoid!" she cried. "Ben is *not* going to hurt me. Besides, there will be at least fifty people there. One in particular who wants to see *you*!"

My stomach flipped. "Shane?"

Rita's eyes were bright and knowing. "He's a fox, isn't he?"

We'd only just met and already my sister knew me so well. I *did* want to see Shane again. Just hearing his name did funny things to my insides.

"Shane asked about you in homeroom this morning," she said. "I told him you'd be at the party. Come on! It will be fun."

I told myself I'd agreed to go only because Rita would go anyway. How could I protect her if she ran off without me? But I couldn't deny the fact that I wanted to see Shane again.

I wore a pair of Rita's worn blue jeans and a T-shirt tie-dyed in bright pink splashes. She'd drawn peace signs on the jeans with a ballpoint pen and patched up the holes in the knees with a flowered print.

"Tuck in the shirt," she instructed. "Wow! My clothes fit you perfectly."

Rita wore jeans too, with a soft green sweater. "We look so much alike," she gasped as we stood side by side in front of the mirror. "I wish Mom could see you."

"Do you think she would like me, Rita?"

"Of course! You're her *daughter*!"

"She gave me away."

Rita hugged me. "She made a mistake. When she sees you, she'll know she was wrong."

"I want to meet our parents, but I don't want them to know who I am. It's too—" I searched for the appropriate word Rita could understand. "*Heavy!* It's way too heavy."

"I can dig that. I think I know of a way you can meet them without them guessing who you are."

She wouldn't tell me any more. She smiled mysteriously and said, "Let me work out the details."

The party was on the beach, and as we walked along the shore I was again struck by the incredible fact that this was a foreign century. The landmarks were the same—the distant jagged blue mountains, the soaring peak of Windy Cliff, the softly curving beach, and the dark, familiar hump of Crab Cave.

My stomach tilted dizzily at the sight of Shane, straddled atop Crab Cave with several of his friends. With their long hair freely blowing in the breeze and their faded bell-bottom jeans, they were the only part of the picture that was out of place, reminding me this was indeed a different century.

Sky arrived with a big silver keg that glinted in the slanting rays of the sinking sun. He called to the boys on the cave, "You guys are going to get me in trouble if you drink in the open! Someone from one of the beach houses might see you and call the cops. Do you want to get me busted for buying alcohol for minors?"

As I watched the boys move to a less conspicuous place behind a giant log, I wished I could tell Sky he shouldn't buy beer for Ben. If Ben didn't get drunk, he might not hurt my sister.

Yet Rita's diary said Ben had eventually gotten his own fake I.D. Apparently, he would find a way to drink with or without Sky.

When Ben arrived, Rita rushed to him. I eyed them nervously as they snuggled up on the pale log beside the keg, Rita's slender arm hooked in Ben's muscular one as she smiled up at him. He looked strong enough to snap my sister's willowy limbs.

I shuddered when Ben caught me watching them. He looked away quickly, his jaw tensing. Did he guess I saw through him?

I was so intent on watching my sister, I didn't notice Shane walk up beside me. "How far can you skip a rock?" he asked, tossing a flat gray stone from hand to hand.

"I don't know," I admitted. "I've never tried it."

"I'm the champion," he said.

"And I suppose you're looking to show off?" I teased and followed him the few steps to the water's edge.

Shane jerked his arm back and snapped his wrist, and the stone skipped over the water, hitting the surface six times before it sank.

"Not bad," I said.

"Not bad?" he asked in mock indignation, raising one eyebrow as he regarded me intently. "Let's see what *you* can do."

I picked up a stone and tried to duplicate his movements. The rock hit the water with a pathetic plop, vanishing instantly.

He pressed a smooth flat stone into my hand and said, "It's all in the wrist," as he helped me position my arm. He smelled good, like soap and fresh salt air. And his touch on my elbow sent a delicious shiver through me. I tossed the stone and it skipped twice before sinking.

"Alright!" he exclaimed, his eyes shining. Soon, I was swept away in those beautiful brown eyes as we flirted and laughed.

I skipped stone after stone, with Shane gently guiding me through each one. I relished the sensation of his warm hand on my arm and the way he dimpled into that gorgeous grin each time I succeeded.

I didn't notice the sun sinking toward the horizon. I didn't hear Rita and Ben get up and walk away. I didn't notice anything but Shane—until I heard my sister scream.

22

I SPUN AWAY FROM THE WATER AND SCANNED THE
group scattered on the logs. *Where was my sister?*

A few kids still hovered around the keg, but Ben
and Rita were missing.

The scream had come from some distance away,
and I took off running in that direction. As I fairly
flew over the rocky shore, a loud pop cracked the air.
It sounded like a gunshot.

He's shot her! He's shot my sister!

I stopped. My stomach heaved. The next seconds
felt like years, and I imagined barnacles could take
root on my shoes as I stood there, too frightened to
move.

What awful sight would greet me around the bend?
The terrible possibilities barely had a chance to

shadow my mind when Rita shrieked, "You little brat!"

She was alive.

Breathless, I raced around the corner and saw Ben and Rita, arms circling each other's waists as they stared up at the wooded hill.

"What happened?" I cried. "I heard you scream and I heard a gun!"

"That wasn't a gun," Ben said. "That was a firecracker."

"I screamed because Chuck threw a sea whip at me," Rita explained, pointing at the hill.

I could barely make out the shape of the little blond boy emerging from the shadows.

"Knock it off, kid," Ben said. "Don't throw any more stuff at us—especially not firecrackers."

"I wasn't throwing them at *you*!" he replied indignantly. "I was throwing them at a bear."

"I don't see any bear," Rita said.

"He swam away," Chuck said. "He escaped from the Woodland Park Zoo after he ate three zookeepers. Now he's probably going to eat you too."

"Stop telling stories, Chuck," she said.

"You can't tell me what to do," he taunted, and scampered up the hill.

"That's my neighbor," Rita explained to me. "He's always popping out of the bushes and scaring me."

"I met him earlier," I said.

A firecracker suddenly exploded at our feet. We all jumped, our eardrums smarting.

"Stop lighting those firecrackers!" Rita yelled. "They aren't toys, Chuck. Somebody could get hurt."

Why did those words sound like a prophecy?

Suddenly I knew. I knew why the warning echoed so eerily and why the little boy was so familiar. He was Mr. Edwards.

A flash of light zipped passed us and another firecracker popped nearby.

"You brat!" Rita screamed.

"Chuck, *please* stop!" I pleaded. "If one of those things blows up in your face, it could blind you."

"I'm not scared," he said. "I have a big box of them. My brother gave them to me before he left for Vietnam. I've already set off a bunch of them."

Mr. Edwards's scarred face and unseeing eyes flashed before me. "Please, Chuck!" I begged. "Please don't set off any more!"

He said, "Mind your own business or I won't let you ride in my helicopter."

"We have to tell his mother," I said, frantically turning to the others.

"Mrs. Addison won't care," Rita said with a shrug. "That kid runs wild."

"What about his dad?" I suggested. "Maybe he can stop him."

"That was Mrs. Addison's first husband—about three husbands ago," she explained. "He's not around anymore. There's no stopping that boy."

"But he could be *hurt*!" I argued.

"It would serve him right," Ben said. "He's such a brat."

I whirled to face him. "You're an uncaring frete!" I cried.

Ben laughed nervously. "I don't know what a frete is, but I don't like your tone."

"It's an Idaho expression," I said. "And *I* don't like your attitude!"

I hadn't planned to spar with a killer. Maybe it wasn't the smartest thing to do. But I hated him so much, I couldn't help it.

"Jenna," Rita said helplessly. *"Please!"* But I was angrily stomping away, pausing only to kick over Ben's beer.

"Hey!" he cried. "Watch what you're doing!"

"Whoops," I said sarcastically. "Was that your beer? I didn't see it."

"What's your problem?" Ben snarled.

"What's *yours*?" I retorted.

Shane came around the bend, confused to find me arguing with his best friend. "Mellow out, you guys," he said and turned to me. "Why did you take off like that?"

"Didn't you hear my sister scream?"

"Girls are always screaming." He sounded unconcerned. "I thought some guy threw his girlfriend in the water or put a crab in her hair."

I was the only one who recognized danger. The only one who knew this night could spell murder. But everyone thought I was paranoid.

For the rest of the evening, Shane watched me curiously as I watched Rita. I didn't dare let her out of my sight again.

I was exhausted from worry when we finally got home. But sleep would not take me. Each time I shut my eyes, an image of a troubled little boy filled my mind. Chuck was heading straight for tragedy and no one cared.

How could I save him? Wasn't there anything I could do?

He was so possessive of the box in the tree house. Was that where he kept his precious firecrackers?

As Rita softly snored, her long hair splayed out on the pillow, I climbed out the window and down the tree. With the moon lighting my way, I found Chuck's tree house and crept up the rope ladder. Just as I suspected, the wooden box stashed in the corner was filled with firecrackers. I lugged the box to the beach and spilled its contents in the surf.

"*Hey!* What are you doing?"

I turned to see Chuck, his mouth contorted in fury.

"It's for your own good," I told him. "You're too young for those things."

"I'm older than *you!*" he said. "I'm nineteen and I'm a midget."

"Yeah, right."

His little face crumpled and he sobbed, "My *brother* gave me those firecrackers!"

Impulsively, my arms reached out to hug him, but he pushed me away. "I hate you!" he said and kicked me.

What could I say to make him understand? I'd just spared him a lifetime of darkness. And made myself into his *enemy*.

"I didn't do it to be mean," I said quietly, but he refused to look at me.

If I went back to 2070, would the elderly Chuck Edwards remember what I did for him? Would he thank me? Or would he still believe that a cruel teenage girl ruined the gift his brother gave him—simply to be mean?

It didn't matter. All that mattered was that Chuck could still see. His mother would not have to turn away when she looked at him. He would not have to be bitter.

As I headed for home, the moon slipped behind the clouds. Immersed in darkness, I walked along the beach, heading unsteadily toward the lights of the houses on the hill. I knew the tide was coming in, for the waves were loud—tumbling furiously as they raced to flood the beach. A sharp, deliberate crunch cut through the persistent rhythm of the waves. *Footsteps!* Was someone following me?

I held my breath and listened. Perhaps it was just someone from one of the beach houses walking his dog. If I couldn't see them, then they couldn't see me. They would probably walk right past me. It would have been reassuring if the footsteps had continued. But they stopped when I did. Someone was standing nearby, listening. *Waiting!*

Maybe it was Chuck tormenting me.

But what if it *wasn't*? The tiny hairs on the back of my neck rose.

I broke into a run. My feet found the wooden steps below Banbury House, and I bounded up them, no longer trying to be quiet. At the top, I raced along the dirt path. Plunging through the shadows, I slammed into something—*someone*! The collision knocked my breath away. Cruel fingers dug into my arms. I looked up into the shadowy face of Ben.

23

"LET GO OF ME!" I CRIED, TWISTING AWAY.

"Then watch where you're going," he said gruffly.

I tried to move past him, but he grabbed my arm. "Wait a minute," he said.

"I have to go home."

"I just want to ask you something." His voice dropped to a hoarse whisper.

I backed away, putting several feet between us. "Don't come any closer," I warned, trying to keep my voice from quavering.

The moon floated free from the clouds, casting an eerie light on Ben's strong features. His eyes seemed to glimmer and I froze, caught in his stare like a frightened deer in bright headlights. The crazy drumming of my own heart filled my ears. My mouth was dry as dust.

Was this the night? Was this the night Ben was supposed to kill my sister? Would he kill me this time, because I was the one who crossed his murderous path?

I was edging away from him when he spoke again. "How come you hate me?"

The question startled me. I cautiously weighed my answer. "You're not good for my sister."

"Why do you say that?"

"You drink too much, Ben."

"You think I'm an *alcoholic*?" he said, laughing much too loudly. "I'm just partying a little. I'm not hurting anybody."

What was I doing, standing there in the dark, trying to reason with a killer?

As he took a drunken step toward me, I dodged out of his way and bolted up the path. I don't think I even breathed again until I'd scrambled up the tree and tumbled through the open window into Rita's room. She muttered something in her sleep as I locked the window.

I crawled deep into my thick sleeping bag, my teeth chattering. I couldn't stop shaking. I wasn't cold. I was frightened. For both of us. *Calm down*, I told myself. But how could I with Ben lurking out there on the path—*stalking us*?

Obviously, he'd been watching the house. If only Rita would believe me!

I should have left him on the beach when he passed out in the water. The tide would have washed in and solved all my problems. *I should have let him drown!*

• • •

In the blazing light of day, I was never as frightened as I was at night. My encounter with Ben faded like a forgotten nightmare as my friends and I celebrated in the school halls on Thursday morning.

"We won!" Rita laughed. "I can't believe those dorks actually backed down."

"They were scared of a lawsuit," Lynn said.

The new dress code allowed girls to wear jeans, as long as they were "tidy with no frayed edges or holes."

I felt heady with the victory. The protest would have eventually taken place without me, yet I liked knowing I'd helped.

I enrolled in school under the name Jenna Mills and vowed to spend my days near my sister. I was assigned to the same homeroom as Rita, along with the rest of those with last names beginning with M through S.

Shane moved his seat next to mine—much to April's disappointment. When he saw me doodling, he asked me to draw something on his notebook. While I sketched a mermaid, we talked. We talked about *everything*—music, parties, school, the dress code. It had never been so easy to talk to a boy before. But eventually the conversation rolled around to Ben.

"I know he's your friend," I said. "But I don't like him. I wish he'd leave my sister alone."

"I don't hear *her* complaining," he said, grinning.

"Ben's a drunk," I spat. "One of these days he'll get so bombed he'll do something he'll regret."

"Wow. You're serious," he said, his velvety brown eyes thoughtful. "I've known Ben forever. He drinks because he's got a rotten home life, but he's an okay guy."

I shivered, wishing Shane knew what I knew. If only I had someone to confide in!

At school, at least, my sister seemed safe. Besides homeroom, we shared four classes and lunch. That meant just two hours I could not guard her.

She and Ben had History class before lunch. He certainly wouldn't murder her with Mr. Frink and a whole class watching!

Still, I was relieved when the school day ended and Rita and I boarded the bus to head for Twin-Star, where she was scheduled for a PK session.

A lab assistant took my sister to a private room for a dice experiment much like the one I'd taken part in.

Sky invited me to wait in his office, a small, untidy room with stale air. "Excuse the mess," he said. "Dr. Crowell split and I haven't had time to clean up after him."

I plucked a framed photograph of a young girl from a box overflowing with junk in the corner. "Who's this?"

"Dr. Crowell's daughter."

"Is this the stuff from his desk?"

Sky nodded. "The old dude finally cracked under the pressure and just took off. He was a genius but undependable."

"Where did he go?"

"Who knows? His wife left him and took the kid

with her. She didn't even tell him where they were moving. Maybe he went to find her."

"He didn't even say good-bye?"

"Did *you*?"

"What?"

"Say good-bye?" he asked, his green eyes burning into mine. "Or did you just *leave*?"

"I just left," I said softly.

His voice brimming with understanding, Sky said, "Maybe I can help you. You must be worried about getting back home."

I gasped. "What do you mean?"

Sky reached into his desk and pulled out a crude version of the visor. "I have spent the last five months immersed in a theory that has convinced me time travel is possible through PK ability and a device like this."

I stared at the visor on the desk, aware my eyes held a glimmer of recognition, aware Sky could read the truth in them.

"I only had to look at you to know you're Rita's sister," he said. "From certain angles, you almost look like twins. And I know for a fact Rita has only two siblings, her brother and the frozen embryo. Did you travel here using a visor like this?"

"Yes," I said, relieved to finally share the truth.

"What year did you travel from?"

"2070."

He whistled softly. "I did it!" His voice held awe. "I really did it. It must have taken years to perfect the visor, but it all began with *my* design."

I tactfully did not point out what Rita had told me, that the invention was actually Dr. Crowell's. I hoped Sky was familiar enough with the visor to help me go home if I wanted to.

"I'm shocked the scientists let you come here, Jenna. I'd think they'd be concerned a visit to the past would challenge the security of their existence. Your visit could have a damaging effect on history as they know it."

"They didn't want me to come," I admitted, and the rest of the story came tumbling out. "Dr. Grady told me it was dangerous. I stole the visor and came here on my own."

"That was a stupid thing to do," Sky said, genuine annoyance sharpening his tone. "You don't know what you got yourself into—"

"You don't understand!" I interrupted. "I *had* to come. I had to stop my sister's murder."

He stared at me in shock as I described Rita's violent death.

"She's like a little sister to me," he said hoarsely. "We've got to help her."

Relief streamed through me as he patted my hand. It felt wonderful to confide in someone, to have someone helping me.

"We'll find a way to keep Rita safe," Sky assured me. "But you must not tell anyone where you came from. Knowledge of the future can be dangerous," he warned. "You could hurt people by telling them too much."

"I wish I could tell Rita and my family!"

"It wouldn't be right," said Sky. "It would change their whole way of thinking. If they didn't like what the future held, they would take a different course in their lives that could have even worse repercussions. Not only would that hurt *them*, it would damage the people from your era. Jenna, you must keep in mind that everything you do has the potential to change the history of the people of 2070."

"I know," I said, sighing in frustration. "Dr. Grady told me the same thing."

"He was right. If you want to return to find the world as you know it, you had better be cautious. Saving Rita, of course, will change things. She may have children and grandchildren who will all make their mark. If your Dr. Grady was here, he'd insist that you go home now without changing Rita's destiny. But I will never forgive myself if that girl is harmed. We'll find a way to save Rita, *without* telling her about time travel."

"How can we stop Ben from hurting her?"

"For starters, *I* won't buy him any more beer," he said. "He should be kept away from alcohol. I'll have a talk with him and encourage him to go to AA meetings. I'm not saying he won't hurt Rita if he's not drunk, but it could make a difference."

Sky drove us home and distracted Rita while I ran up to the attic to get the visor. He had promised to examine it and advise me on the best way to use it—*if* I chose to go back to the future.

My loyalties were torn. Rita needed me. But thoughts of the mother who raised me had begun to surface as my anger toward her gradually wore thin. She was wrong to lie to me. Yet now I understood how a person could lie to someone she loved. I, after all, had lied to Rita.

I was only trying to protect my sister. Had Mom been trying to protect *me*?

Mom had been on my mind that morning when Rita asked, "Why do you look so sad?"

"I was thinking about my mom," I'd told her. "She's probably worried."

"Does she know you're here?"

"No."

"You could call her."

Of course I couldn't.

Had time stood still since I'd left? How long had I been gone? The three days spent here, or only seconds?

I felt a sudden stab of regret. Why had I left on such bad terms? Mom must be going crazy with worry. Or was another Jenna still *there* in 2070? Was I living parallel lives?

It was all very confusing.

I pulled the trunk away from the corner and reached behind it. My fingers felt only the dusty wood of the attic floor. The visor was gone.

24

WHO IN THE WORLD COULD HAVE TAKEN THE VISOR? Whoever found it certainly wouldn't have known what it was!

Frantically, I searched the attic, digging through old suitcases and knocking over boxes until Sky tooted his horn and I drifted back outside and numbly reported, "It's gone."

Sky stared at me, his words weighed with disbelief as he said, "You wouldn't misplace something that important, Jenna."

"What was it?" Rita asked.

"A visor," I admitted, too upset to think up another lie. Without the visor, I no longer had the option of returning home.

Rita's forehead crinkled in confusion. "A *visor*? Like the one at Twin-Star?"

Sky leapt in and covered for me. "It was an updated visor," he said quickly. "I gave it to Jenna the other day so she could experiment. You guys are so much alike, I thought she might have PK skills too."

"Why didn't you tell me?" Rita asked, hurt.

"It was a surprise," I said miserably. Losing the visor was bad enough without having to tell more lies. I hated deceiving my sister.

"It couldn't have walked away on its own," Sky said. "You've *got* to find it."

I turned to Rita. "Ask Jim and our parents if they've seen it."

Despite an intense search, the visor did not turn up.

If I couldn't go home, could I stay with the Mills family? Would they accept me as a sister and daughter?

Perhaps I was *meant* to stay here. Without the visor, I did not have to choose between two centuries. I could stay forever and live out my life with my real family.

Though Sky had warned it was dangerous, I still longed to meet the rest of my family.

I watched our brother from Rita's window seat as he and Chuck played croquet in the grassy backyard. Jimmy gingerly swung the croquet club, his head bowed in concentration. Caught in a shaft of sunlight, his curls gleamed like fire.

"Where did Jimmy get all that red hair?" I asked.

"Grandma Mills had red hair before it turned gray."

Grandma Mills! How lucky my sister was to have

grandparents—to have blood relatives who knew and loved her. Would I get a chance to know them too?

"Jimmy and Grandma Mills both have fiery tempers," Rita continued. "It must come with the red hair. Jimmy drives me up the wall. Sometimes he—"

"He *loves* you!" I interrupted. I pictured our brother, gray and frail from the years, eyes glistening with tears as he remembered his sister's tragic death.

"He'd gag if he heard you say that," said Rita. "The only thing Jimmy loves is his bike!"

"That's not true."

"How would *you* know?" she asked, amused. "You've never met him!"

"I wish I could! I wish I could meet our parents!"

Friday night my wish came true.

"We're going to a party," Rita informed me. I sat on her bed as she did my makeup, insisting, "No peeking until I'm done."

"It seems like you're putting an awful lot on," I protested. "Usually I just wear a little eye makeup and lip color."

"This is just foundation," she said, rubbing her fingers over my face as her eyes danced with a secret. "It's practically invisible."

"Where's the party?"

"It's a surprise. Now close your mouth while I paint your lips."

When she was done, she still wouldn't let me near the mirror. "Come on!" she said and grabbed my hand, pulling me into the hallway and down the stairs.

"Rita, wait!" I said. "What if our parents see—"

"Surprise!" a chorus of voices rose from the bottom of the stairs. Dozens of people milled about, laughing up at us.

"Happy birthday, Jenna!" someone shouted, and I turned to see our mother, smiling at me—*looking right at me!*

"Rita," I hissed. "Does she *know* who I am?"

"All she knows is you're a friend from school and this is your birthday," said Rita, turning me to face the oval mirror on the hallway wall. My face was painted like a clown's, my skin milk-white, my lips thick and red. Orange triangles decorated my cheeks. No one could possible recognize me.

"Pretend it's your birthday," Rita whispered. "I told them you loved costume parties. It's the only way I could think for you to meet them."

As we descended the steps, I realized everyone was in costume. Sky was clad in pirate's garb, a red scarf on his head, a patch over one eye, and a plastic parrot fastened to his shoulder.

April was a flower child, with strings of beads draped around her neck and a daisy painted on one cheek.

Our parents were cowboys and Jimmy wore a Spider-man mask.

"Ben thinks costume parties are corny, so he's not coming," said Rita. "And I didn't invite Shane because it might be awkward with April here, since she likes him too. Don't tell her, but Shane and Ben are going to meet us in Seattle tomorrow and spend the day with us."

Rita bounded upstairs to change into her gypsy costume while I mingled with our guests, greeting some of the kids from school as I snaked through the crowd toward my parents.

My mother ducked into the kitchen and I followed her on rubbery legs. All the wind seemed to leave my lungs and my voice was barely audible as I said, "It's nice of you to have the party here, Mrs. Mills."

Smiling warmly, she took off her cowboy hat, and her shiny chestnut hair—so much like mine—spilled free. I caught my breath, searching her face for a sign of my own. It was odd seeing my nose planted square in the middle of unfamiliar features.

"Are you new in town, Jenna?"

"Yes, but my relatives have lived here a long time."

"I hope you like lemon cake with white frosting," she said, taking a square white bakery box from the refrigerator.

"Thank you!" I cried, overwhelmed by emotion.

"It's nothing."

"Can I see some of your pottery?" I asked.

Her eyes brightened with pride and she led me to a corner of the kitchen where a shelf held dozens of tall vases, squat mugs, and oblong ashtrays.

"Very nice," I said, genuinely impressed—not so much by the pieces themselves but by the fact that *my* mother's hands had shaped them.

I could have stood forever in that spot, listening to her low, silky voice as she talked about her art. But someone yelled that Jimmy had knocked over the punch bowl and she rushed away to clean up the mess.

I gently stroked a vase. My fingertips fit into the grooves she'd pressed into the rim. Were my hands like hers? I'd forgotten to notice.

The mother who raised me did not have a creative bone in her body. Now I knew where my artistic streak came from.

"Where's the cake?"

I turned to see my brother, his mask pushed off his face as he shoved potato chips into his mouth.

"I've been wanting to meet you," I said.

"Oh, hi. Bye!"

"Wait!" I touched his arm and turned him toward me. His eleven-year-old skin was still baby soft and he smelled like freshly mowed grass. I gently stroked the curls as *he* had stroked my hair with his withered fingers on Deep Brine Island.

"You're nuts!" he exclaimed and bolted from the room.

"What did you expect?" Rita asked, appearing in the doorway, clad in a flowing gypsy skirt, silver bracelets jingling on her slender arms.

"He'll grow up nice," I said. "And Mother is *wonderful*!"

"Not when you live with her. Don't get me wrong. I love her, but she's awfully wrapped up in herself."

"She's an *artist*! She's so creative. I think it's frazzin—um—I mean, far out."

"It's kind of cool," Rita said. "But hardly anyone buys her pottery."

My sister could not appreciate what she had, simply because she'd *always* had it. She did not understand how it felt to be the missing piece of a jigsaw puzzle. My family was a big, colorful flesh and blood puzzle with all of its parts intact—except for one forgotten piece. *Me!*

I floated into the living room, studying my family's faces. My father was standing in the dining room doorway, handing a glass of wine to a tubby neighbor man who had wandered over from across the street to join the party. Tall and lanky with a wide nose and kind blue eyes, my father looked like an interesting man, but he did not resemble me. Yet, as I watched, *my* smile curled on his face.

Thin lips. Slightly lopsided. Stretching easily into a wide grin.

My smile! Out of place, yet so heart-wrenchingly familiar on his angular, masculine face.

What would he say if he knew I was his daughter?

"You folks were fortunate to get such a great house with a water view," the neighbor told my father.

"We lucked out with a wise investment that allowed us to purchase it when we were first married," he replied.

I stood at my father's elbow, wishing he would turn around and notice me. But he was caught up in talk of real estate investments.

"Jenna," my mother called. "There's a boy at the door to see you."

With a last wistful glance at the father who might

never know me, I went to the door to find Shane. "Is that *you*?" he asked, laughing.

"Oh!" My fingers went to my face. I'd forgotten about my costume and felt myself blushing under my makeup.

"I heard it was your birthday and wanted to give you this."

"It's the shell we found on the beach!" I exclaimed in delight. The small swirling shell was now strung on a delicate gold chain.

"To remind you of the night we met," Shane said quietly and slipped it over my head. I stared at him, speechless.

Suddenly embarrassed, he shrugged and said, "It's no big deal. It's just an old chain my sister used to wear."

"It's great," I said. "Thank you!"

He declined my invitation to come in, explaining that Ben was waiting in the car. I peeked around Shane and saw Ben's car, a chunky shadow sputtering noisily in the dark driveway. Ben was quietly sitting in the dark, watching our romantic scene in the lit doorway—probably with an evil smirk on his face!

I shuddered as I watched them drive off. It was the first present a boy had given me and Ben was *not* going to spoil it for me! I pressed the shell to my cheek and sighed. Shane had tried to minimize the gift, but it wasn't easy for boys to admit their feelings. Obviously, the night we met *meant* something to him! Would it be a date we would celebrate in the years to come?

Or would I find the visor and go home to Kyle? The memory of my other boyfriend sent a big gangly shadow of guilt hopscotching through my conscience.

It was as if I had two lives and couldn't choose between them. Here, I had my real parents and a sister and brother and *Shane*! But in 2070, the mother who raised me would surely be missing me. And then there was Kyle . . .

Whirling with the choices, I drifted into the kitchen where my mother was sponging off the counter. If only I could tell her about my predicament! My real flesh and blood mother would surely know what to do!

"Shane's a doll," she said with a knowing grin.

"I've never met anyone like him," I admitted.

"Makes me wish *I* were twenty years younger."

"He made me this necklace from a shell we found the night we met," I confided. "He's so sweet. I think I'm starting to love him." My words fell to a whisper and unexpected tears scorched my eyes. "I don't want to leave him."

She studied me so intently, I thought for a moment she'd recognized me, despite the fact I was hidden beneath layers of clown makeup.

Oh, Mother! I cried silently. *Please see me!* Surely something in my eyes would tell her I was her daughter.

In the long moment she stared at me, hope spread its soft wings, fluttering in my chest. My mother—my *real* mother was giving me her undivided attention. I ached to throw my arms around her and tell her who I was.

Encouraged by her interest, I blurted, "I have a problem. A *big* problem."

"Sounds serious."

"It is. I don't know where to live. I care about people in two different places—a *long* way apart. If I go home, I'll never see Shane and some of my relatives again. If I stay here, I have no place to live. And people back home will miss me."

I sucked in my breath as she seemed to ponder my predicament, her eyes flickering thoughtfully. I half expected her to invite me to live with them.

"I know what my next project's going to be," she said suddenly.

"Huh?"

"Clowns!" She laughed and clapped her hands. "It came to me a minute ago when you got teary-eyed. You know the cliché about clowns? Laughing on the outside, crying on the inside? Well, I could do a mug that was a happy clown on the outside, and when you looked inside the cup, he'd be crying."

Dumbfounded, I stared at her. Hadn't she been listening to me?

"It's kind of corny," she continued. "But clown pottery could make a profound statement."

"Great idea," I heard myself say.

"Oh, and don't feel bad about your boyfriend, honey. Believe me, you'll think you're in love a dozen more times before you turn twenty. Puppy love is all part of being a teenager. You'll forget Shane and be chasing some other boy a week after you're back home."

A tight knot of sadness froze in my chest. The cold spread, creeping through my limbs until the tips of my fingers and toes turned to ice.

My mother moved to a table in the corner and began shaping a slab of clay. She hummed to herself, intent on the red clay oozing between her fingers.

At that moment, I knew it would not matter if I washed off my clown makeup. My mother would not know me. Even if she recognized I was of her flesh, she could not *see* me.

A bitter taste rose in my throat as I watched her playing with that clay. How could she have left me in a freezer all those years? How could she have gone and lived her life and died without knowing me?

She must have known I'd be born someday, too late for me to know her!

It was at that instant the meaning of my father's words to the neighbor hit me: *"We lucked out with a wise investment . . ."* He meant *me!*

As Jim had told me on Deep Brine Island, our biological parents sold me and bought Banbury House with the proceeds.

My father did not seem like a cruel man. Surely he would not have made that comment if he'd known the daughter he'd put on ice was standing right beside him.

Perhaps if I introduced myself to my biological parents, they would make an effort to know and love me. But I found myself thinking, *Why should I give them the chance*? They'd made their choices and were content with the outcome.

My blood flowed through the veins of Steven and Bonnie Mills. Some of my features had first sprouted on their faces. And, yes, *I did* feel a connection when I looked at those faces.

But *another* face flashed before me. A kind and gentle face, violet eyes brimming with love. Suddenly, I felt an excruciating bond with the woman who had raised me. *She* was my mother. I did not have her circular face, her methodical walk, or her simple logic. Yet she gave me life and loved me every day of that life.

I'd turned my back on her, not even bothering to make things right before I went away. Perhaps *forever.*

Oh, Mom! I'm so sorry I hurt you!

What if I couldn't find the visor? Would I ever see my mother again?

I cornered Sky on the front porch, where he leaned on the railing, staring out into the night.

I said, "Once Rita is safe, I want to go home. My mother's got to be going crazy with worry!"

"I'll try to help you," he said, his voice low and concerned. "But without the visor—"

"Maybe Dr. Crowell can help," I blurted. "Is there any way to find him?"

He stared at the floor. I'd insulted him.

"Please don't take this wrong," I said quickly. "I'm sure Dr. Crowell couldn't have invented the visor without your help. But you know the old saying—two heads are better than one."

"You've got a point. I'll write to his p.o. box and tell him about you. Hopefully, he's having his mail forwarded to wherever he is. When he hears the visor worked, I'm pretty sure he'll come back."

I sat down on a wicker chair, relief flowing through me. Then something occurred to me. If Dr. Crowell returned and claimed rightful credit for the visor, what would become of Sky? And *Kyle?*

Would Sky be destined to fetch the coffee forever? Without the prestige of being an inventor, would he still attract Kyle's grandmother?

What if I returned to my time and Kyle had not been born?

25

SATURDAY MORNING BROUGHT RAIN. MY SISTER didn't mind. She tilted her head back, laughing up at the sky as the silver drops splashed down on her, plastering her tie-dyed T-shirt to her body.

We'd taken the bus to downtown Seattle, and now we were headed along the wet sidewalk, on our way to meet Ben and Shane.

Rita leapt into a puddle, splattering us both and then twirled about gleefully. That was an interesting thing about kids in this era. They seemed to revel in nature—even if it was soaking them to the skin.

Teenagers in 2070 were generally more reserved, buttoning up against the cold and avoiding everything but the most comfortable of conditions. Kyle would think Rita had brain-drag if he could see her dancing along the sidewalk, raindrops glistening on her forehead, her hair in wet ringlets. But I got into the spirit of things, singing with her as we strolled along.

My sister's good mood faded when we plopped down at the counter next to Shane and he told us, "I don't know what happened to Ben. He's probably out drinking."

I, of course, was relieved. The less Ben was around, the better! But Rita's face fell and she said three was a crowd and maybe she should just go home. "Please stay," I pleaded.

Despite the fact I would have loved to have been alone with Shane—who looked gorgeous in a fringed suede jacket that matched his eyes—I wasn't letting Rita out of my sight. It was simply too dangerous. So the three of us headed for Seattle Center. "I want to go up in the Space Needle," I'd told them.

The truth was, I wanted to keep my promise to Suki. I'd found her mother in the yellow pages of the Mills' phone book. Madame Trudy Calacort read tarot cards in the corner of a bookstore near the Seattle Center.

Shane had parked his car in a nearby parking lot, but we were just a half mile from our destination, so we decided to walk. When we passed the bookstore, I pretended interest in a book displayed in the window. Inside, as Rita and Shane became engrossed in the books, I slipped to the back of the store.

"What would you like to know?" Madame Calacort asked, shuffling cards with deft but stubby fingers and gazing at me through pale blue eyes so much like Suki's I gasped in surprise.

I sat down at the wobbly card table and said, "Actually, I have something to tell *you*."

She possessed the confidence Suki lacked. It showed on her heart-shaped face as she brushed away a lock of blond hair and appraised me with a sweeping glance.

"You have a daughter," I blurted. "And she forgives you!"

"You must have mistaken me with someone else," she said crisply. "I have no children."

"Your daughter, Suki, will be born a century from now. She'll have your eyes and blond hair."

"Are you on drugs or something?" she asked suspiciously.

"I'm psychic like you. I know things about the future. Is that so hard to believe?"

"Look, I'm tired of you teenagers coming in here and making a joke out of my tarot cards. This is my job and I don't have time to—"

"Suki will have another distinct trait," I interrupted. "Her eyes will be wide and blue, but not *exactly* like yours. There is something unique about them she must have inherited from another relative. Her pupils have jagged edges."

Realization crept reluctantly over her face and she blurted, "My father had jagged pupils!"

"Your daughter inherited them—or rather, she *will*! Suki will be very lonely because she'll be raised by uncaring scientists. But she said to tell you she forgives you for selling her embryo."

Madame Calacort bounded from her chair. "Who

are you?" she bellowed. "Why are you tormenting me?"

"It doesn't matter. I kept my promise to Suki!"

Unsatisfied with my response, she barreled toward me and her long red skirt ripped as it caught on a nail on a bookshelf.

"Who sent you?" she cried, her oniony breath hot on my face. "Who told you about my father's eyes?"

Sharp fingernails sunk into my wrist. I jerked away, but she lunged at me, the bookshelf still hooked to her skirt. The shelf toppled over and as books thudded to the floor, I turned and fled, flying past Shane and Rita, who followed me outside.

"What was *that* all about?" Rita asked me as we hurried across the street.

"I don't know. She must be crazy!" I said shakily, and stole a glance over my shoulder. The black window of the bookshop winked strangely in the gray day's light, like an evil eye, watching me scornfully.

"Let's skip the Space Needle," I said. "Just *looking* at it makes me dizzy!"

I wanted to get as far away from Madame Calacort as possible!

"Let's ride the ferry to Bainbridge Island," Rita suggested. "Sometimes we stay on it all day, riding back and forth."

The ferry was several stories high and roomy enough for hundreds of people. But this day only a sprinkling of travelers roamed about or lounged on some of the dozens of long vinyl seats by the windows.

As we pulled away from Seattle, Rita strolled off by herself. For the first time, I felt safe letting her out of my sight. How in the world could Ben hurt her when she was on a boat in the middle of Puget Sound?

Shane took my hand and led me to the ferry's outside lower deck where we watched the hazy blue-green landscape glide by. We stood shoulder to shoulder, feeling the brisk salty breeze blow off the water. The wind was so strong it snatched our breath away when we faced it. So we turned toward each other and soon we were kissing. Our hair streamed behind us, gold and chestnut strands mingling together in the breeze.

I snuggled into the warmth of Shane's arms, wishing I'd been born in this time, wishing I could stay forever and maybe—someday—marry him. We'd buy a farm and while he was planting and watching green things grow, I would create breathtaking paintings in a studio set up in the corner of our barn with the cows looking over my shoulder.

The perfect little picture frayed at the edges and blurred. How could I enjoy my life knowing I'd hurt the only mother I'd ever known?

I'd find a way to get back to her. My decision was made. But it weighed like a pile of rocks in the middle of my stomach.

"You want coffee or something?" Shane asked. "There's a snack bar here on the ferry."

We'd reached the island and stayed on the boat, which was now heading back toward Seattle. While

Shane went to get drinks, I checked on Rita. She was outside on the upper deck, still stung because Ben had stood her up. She stared out at the shrinking, forested island, tears trickling down her face.

I touched her shoulder. "You're better off without him."

"How do you know?" she sobbed angrily. "How can you be so *sure* about your premonition? If you're so psychic, what am I thinking right now?"

"I don't know," I admitted.

"That's what I *thought*! You don't know Ben. And you don't know anything about our relationship!"

Frustration bubbled up inside me. I'd gone through so much to help her and she would not let me! Rita was on a full-speed track toward tragedy and she would not listen to her own sister.

Suddenly, I couldn't stand it. "I *do* know!" I cried, and the whole story came gushing out—from my discovery of her diary to my trip back in time.

She stared at me through eyes flat with disbelief. Her expression unnerved me. Unflinching. Coldly calm. The stillness of her face starkly contrasted with the wildness of her long hair whipping in the wind.

Finally she spoke. "You must think I'm pretty gullible."

"I wouldn't lie to you about this! We're *sisters*!"

She laughed bitterly. "You lied before, how do I know you're not lying now? How do I know you're *really* my sister?" With that, she whirled away in a huff.

Deflated, I watched her go.

"There you are," Shane said and handed me a steaming cup of coffee. I followed him inside, where we sat gazing out at the wide expanse of rippling gray water. "Someday a man-made island will float here," I said. "It will be populated with old people and full of pink buildings that glow in the sunlight."

"You're a trippy chick!"

"I'm serious."

Sky had warned me about revealing the truth. But I had already broken my vow to keep my secret and my own sister had not believed me. Maybe it was selfish, but I needed someone I cared about to believe me.

When I told Shane my story, his response, like Rita's, was disbelief.

I ticked off the names of the presidents in the years to come. "Twenty years from now, you'll remember this conversation and know I told the truth!"

Then I realized my visit here might have set off a chain reaction that could affect who became president. So I said, "Mt. St. Helens will erupt in 1980. Think of me when that happens."

"Maybe we'll be together then," he said, a twinkle in his eye. He still thought I was kidding.

"I may be leaving soon, Shane. You might never see me again. If there is a way to get back to my time, I'll have to go."

His face reflected pain. "If you're really going away, please don't play this game with me. You don't have to make up some crazy fantasy. If you're leaving, we could write to each other."

"No we can't."

"Do you have another boyfriend?" he asked hoarsely. "Is that it?"

"No one I like as much as you," I said softly. "I'll never forget you."

Lost in the moment and his eyes, I didn't notice the ferry had stopped. The Seattle skyline was no longer a jagged line in the distance. The buildings loomed above us as people trickled off the boat.

"Where's Rita?" I cried. "Did she get off?"

"I don't know. I thought she wanted to ride back and forth for a while."

I leapt up and bounded up the green metal stairs to the top deck where I'd last seen my sister. I looked toward shore where the faded gray dock was already growing smaller, and there, amidst the crowd, I recognized a pair of slumped shoulders and long brown hair.

"Rita!" I cried. "Rita, please wait for us to get back!"

But my voice was lost in the wind.

26

THERE WAS NOTHING TO DO BUT WAIT OUT THE hour and ten minutes it would take for the ferry to return to Seattle.

"Hey, don't look so upset," Shane said and hugged me as we watched the Seattle skyline shrink. "Rita needs time alone. She'll be okay."

I wished I could believe that. But I knew I had let my sister down. If Ben found her . . .

I could not finish the thought. Why hadn't I watched her more carefully?

The trip passed with excruciating slowness, and when the ferry once again nudged the Seattle dock I hurried off.

I declined Shane's invitation to see a matinee. When he dropped me off at Banbury House, I practically flew from the car.

"Rita!" I cried, charging up the stairs. "Rita, are you here?"

I threw open her bedroom door. Her daisy-patterned bedspread was pulled taut over her bed, and the heaps of clothes no longer littered the floor. Apparently, she'd come home, cleaned her room, and left. The house echoed emptily as I dashed back down the stairs.

Had she gone to the beach? That's where I went when I needed to think.

I headed out the back door and down the path. A salty wind fiercely shook the Scotch broom bushes clinging to the hillside. Huddling into my jacket, I leaned into the wind.

"There's the girl who thinks she's so smart!" an irate voice slurred.

I spun around to see Ben, staggering along the path behind me, his eyes small and red. He drank from a bottle of whiskey and swore at me drunkenly.

"Where's my sister?"

He laughed. "You tell me. Out with some other guy probably. I'd like to find her . . ."

"No!" I shrieked, and leapt around him.

I lunged up the hill to Banbury House and burst through the back door. My hands were shaking so badly I could barely dial the phone.

"Sky!" I cried at the sound of his warm voice. "Ben's drunk! I think this is the day he'll hurt Rita! We've got to find her!"

"Take it easy," he said firmly. "I'll look for your

sister. You keep an eye on Ben. But promise me you won't let him see you. He could hurt you too, Jenna."

"I'll crawl along the bank and watch him. If I stay in the bushes, he won't see me."

"On second thought, this is too dangerous," Sky said. "Stay in the house and lock the doors. I'll find Rita and bring her straight home."

"But she could be wandering along the beach. Ben could find her first. I'll be careful."

"I don't know—"

"We're wasting time, Sky!"

"Okay. I'll see if she's at the burger place by the school. If you see Ben approach Rita, start screaming and don't stop until you've got the attention of the whole neighborhood."

My heart thudding, I scrambled down the path until I spotted Ben on the beach. I was prepared to follow him, but he wasn't going anywhere. He'd settled down on a log, swigging from the bottle.

I sat shivering on the wooden stairs which led to the beach. Perched there, I could watch Ben and a wide expanse of shore. If Rita approached him, I'd see her before she got close.

It's strange how ridiculous details can float up into your consciousness in the middle of a crisis. I found myself thinking about the stairs I sat on, and how well built they were. They were the same steps that existed in my century—although in my time they were worn to a winter gray by the endless salt breeze and the thousands of beachcombers who had tromped over them.

I relaxed a little, sagging against the hard wood of the steps as Ben stretched out on the sand, apparently napping. His body was so still it seemed almost lifeless. I shuddered, remembering another still body on the beach. Mr. Edwards must have lain there just like that. My eyes shifted, involuntarily seeking the deadly ledge of Windy Cliff. Startled, I realized I could not see Windy Cliff from the steps.

That can't be! I thought, leaping to my feet.

Kyle had said he was on the steps when Mr. Edward fell. He claimed he *saw* him fall.

It made no sense. The stairs were in the same place and the landscape had not changed. Kyle could not possibly have seen Mr. Edwards fall from here.

With creeping dread, I realized Kyle had lied.

27

WHY WOULD KYLE LIE? HE WAS AN HONEST PERSON.
I must have misunderstood. Yet a horrible possibility
snaked through my mind. What if *Kyle* pushed Mr.
Edwards off the cliff?

But that was *crazy*. Why would he kill a helpless
old man? I no sooner asked myself the question and
the answer was there—in the form of more questions.

Suppose Mr. Edwards was a threat. He was always
talking about Rita's murder. Did he know something
Kyle did not want publicized?

In a cold rush, my brother's words on Deep Brine
Island came back to me: "Those idiot defense attorneys tried every trick in the book to get that killer off
the hook. First they dragged in an unreliable witness
and put him on the stand—a neighbor boy who was a

known liar and couldn't possibly have seen the killing."

Couldn't possibly have seen . . .

"Couldn't have seen because he was *blind*!" I whispered.

With an icy certainty, I realized Chuck Edwards was the witness for the defense in Ben's murder trial—a little blind boy who liked to spy on people. Chuck must have *heard* the murder.

A young Charles Edwards witnessed the murder and a hundred years later was still talking about it. But why would that bother Kyle, unless he had something to hide?

Like a sudden flash of lightning, Kyle's words slashed through my mind. "On his deathbed, my grandfather told me how he made our family what it is," he'd said. "Things were much more complicated than I'd thought."

"Oh my God!" I cried. Numb with shock, I stumbled down the steps. "Wake up, Ben!"

"What do *you* want?" he slurred.

"Where did you get that bottle?" I demanded.

"Why do you want to know?"

"Ben, if you really care about Rita, then *tell* me. She's in danger!"

"Yeah, she told me. You think I'm going to kill her."

"I was wrong. Please tell me who gave you the bottle."

"Sky."

The answer confirmed my worst fear.

Sky wanted Ben drunk!

"Sky confessed everything to his grandson on his deathbed," I said. "He killed Rita and blamed it on you! We've got to stop him before he does it again. He's looking for her now. He might have already found her!"

"You're not making sense."

"He's going to hurt her!"

"What?" Ben stared at me through watery blood-shot eyes. "Why would he do that?"

"Because of the visor!" I cried.

But Ben had passed out. I knelt beside him, frantically shaking his arm. "Ben, listen to me! Sky is taking credit for the visor and other inventions. The whole Mettley family got rich off those inventions. But Rita could blow everything for them. She's the only one who knows he didn't really invent the visor."

"Not the *only* one!" a sharp voice interrupted.

I whirled around, my breath snagging in my throat at the sight of the gun in Sky's hand. "You could blow things for me too, dear," he said evenly.

"Where's my sister?"

"Don't worry. You girls will get to say good-bye to each other. Turn around and start walking."

I glanced at Ben.

"He can't help you now," Sky said. "He's out cold."

I winced with fear as the gun poked sharply into my back. Sky instructed me to head toward the base of the bank where we were concealed from the view of the houses on the hill. I stumbled ahead of him as we continued south along the shore.

Sharp claws of terror gripped my stomach. Should I run? Would he shoot me right then and there if I did?

As we neared Crab Cave, he hesitated. "Sit down on that log," he ordered.

"You can't get away with this, Sky!"

"Apparently, I already did. According to you, Ben got blamed for Rita's murder last time around."

"What about *my* murder? Who will you blame *that* on?"

"As far as the authorities are concerned, you don't exist. Your parents aren't going to report you missing. You're still in the freezer at Twin-Star and won't be born in their lifetime. In fact, you might not be born at all. Wouldn't it be a shame if the power went out and the frozen embryo melted?"

"You can't do that!" I said. "I'll never be born!"

"Come to think of it, that building did look awfully dark when I drove by. I wonder what could have caused the power failure."

He was going to kill me twice!

"Lie down with your face to the ground," he said coldly.

"Think about what you're doing," I pleaded. "Things could be different this time. You said so yourself! My trip to the past may have already changed your fate. Remember, you wrote to Dr. Crowell and told him about me. He might come back now. You won't be able to steal his inventions and you will have killed two people for nothing!"

An amused smile twitched on his lips. "Nice try. But Dr. Crowell will *not* be back."

"You sent him the letter!"

"He'll never read it." His eyes glazed over and I followed his stare to Crab Cave. "You didn't know about his murder?" he asked. "I must have hid him well."

I gasped. "His body is in *there*? Is that why you asked the boys to move away from the cave that night at the party, because you had a body hidden in there—because you *killed* Dr. Crowell?"

"Three weeks ago. You mean to tell me the authorities never found him?"

"They found him—right where you buried him in Crab Cave after you put a bullet in his head," I said flatly. "But they never figured out who he was. You must have been about a hundred years old by the time they pulled the skeleton out of the cave."

Sky's eyes lit up and he whistled softly. "A *hundred*? So I can look forward to a long and prosperous life?"

I was sorry I'd told him. It was not the way to talk him out of murder.

He smiled, gloating over the dazzling future that stretched before him. With a smug confidence, he looked away. I seized the opportunity and grabbed a sea whip. I swung it at him and it connected with the gun, knocking it from his grasp.

As he bent to pick up the gun, I rolled over the log and tore into the underbrush along the bank. Sharp stickers scraped my face and snagged my clothes as I raced up the hill, hidden by the dense growth.

"You little witch!" Sky yelled.

Afraid to stop, afraid to look back, I propelled myself forward, squeezing between shrubs, scrambling over fallen logs, and racing around trees.

"I'll get you!" he shouted. The threat crackled with hate, but the volume had faded.

Had I lost him? It sounded as if he was heading in the other direction. Fueled by hope, I plowed forward. Somewhere nearby was the shortcut Shane had shown me. If I could find it, I'd run to Main Street, wave down a car, and go to the police.

But a wild thrashing in the bushes warned me Sky was back on my trail. *Dangerously close!*

My skin prickled at the sound of his enraged roar and I stumbled forward. Suddenly, I was faced with a wall of blackberry bushes, with thorns so sharp they would shred me to ribbons if I tried to go through them.

I backtracked, glancing around wildly, searching for a hiding place. And then I saw it.

Chuck's tree house.

Frantically, I climbed up the rope ladder and pulled it up after me.

"What are *you* doing here?"

I whirled to see Chuck, his lower lip thrust out belligerently. "Get out!" he shouted.

I clamped my hand over his mouth and hissed, "There's a man with a gun out there who will kill us both if he finds us."

Chuck's eyes widened and I slowly removed my hand.

"Wow!" he said, his voice full of awe. "I'm going to kill him before he can kill us."

"Shh!"

"I can do it," he whispered. "I have a space weapon."

"This is no time for games."

"I'm not making it up," he insisted. He reached into his box and pulled out the missing visor. "See? It shoots out rays when you turn it on. I bet it could kill somebody."

"My visor! You stole it from the attic!"

"So? You took my firecrackers. Now we're even-steven."

How much fuel was left? Enough to get home? I could try to go back to 2070. I could put on the visor and return to save my own life!

With the visor hugging my head, I relaxed my body, trying to picture 2070.

"I'm going to find you!" Sky's angry voice shrieked.

If I went back now, I would have accomplished nothing. My sister would still die. And Ben—poor, misunderstood Ben—would be executed for her murder!

What if I went in the *other* direction—back just a few hours, just far enough back in time to warn Rita about Sky?

But if I did that, I might use the last of the fuel. I might never be able to return to my time.

I've got to save my sister, I thought and squeezed

my mind, trying to visualize an earlier hour in the day. *8 a.m. I'm waking up! The day is just beginning . . .*

"I know you're up there!" Sky's enraged shout shattered my concentration.

My heart turned to ice as a branch creaked with Sky's weight.

"He's climbing the tree!" Chuck cried.

I must clear my mind of the here and now, I ordered myself. *I must concentrate on another time!*

Shane's kiss. The memory of it was still tingling on my lips. I desperately grabbed at that moment—trying vainly to transport myself back a few hours to when I was safe in his arms.

Evil laughter echoed off the rickety walls of the tree house, and my eyes flew open. Sky's head had poked through the opening of the floor, and he grinned at me triumphantly.

I forced my eyes shut and willed myself to think only of Shane's soft lips pressing against mine. As I blocked out all else, the memory grew vivid—so vivid it was *real*.

I was kissing Shane, and his strong arms were around me. His hand slid up my back and he gently stroked my hair. "Hey!" he said, fingering the visor. "Where did this thing on your head come from?"

We were standing on the ferry deck, watching the soft blue hills pass in the distance. "Oh, Shane!" I cried. "You're *real*! I'm really here with you!"

"Wow. My kisses have never had *this* effect on anybody before. You're trembling."

"It's the cold air," I said, turning my face to the breeze. I took off the visor and tucked it in my purse.

He kissed me again, and I felt electrified. Our lips pulled apart, and he shook his head. "I just had the weirdest feeling I've lived this moment before. What do they call that? Déjà vu?"

"We *have* lived this moment before—just three hours ago. Someday there will be an island here, with pink buildings that glow in the sun. But I guess I wasn't supposed to tell you that until about an hour from now."

"You're a trippy chick," he said with a grin.

"You don't know the half of it," I told him, and launched into my tale of time travel.

I didn't have to search for Rita. I knew she'd be on the upper deck, crying over Ben. "Rita," I said as she fixed her red eyes on me, "I want to talk to you about Ben."

"I'm sick of your premonitions! If you're so psychic—"

"Then why don't you tell me what I'm thinking right now," I finished for her.

She gasped in surprise.

"I'm not a mind reader, Rita. I lied to you. I was only trying to protect you. I made a mistake—a *big* mistake. Ben has his problems, but he's no killer. Someone else is going to hurt you. It's a long story, and I hope you'll believe me even though I haven't been completely truthful before."

When the ferry reached Seattle, the three of us got

off together and I dashed to the nearest phone booth and called the police.

"There is a body in Crab Cave on Banbury Beach," I said. "It is Dr. Crowell, a scientist at Twin-Star Labs. He was shot by Sky Mettley, his assistant. He killed him so he could take credit for Dr. Crowell's inventions."

"Who is this?" the detective asked suspiciously.

"I'm sorry. I can't tell you. Just look in the cave."

We watched Sky on the six o'clock news, his face stark white, his eyes wild with confusion as the police led him away. He had no memory, of course, of our encounter on the beach, for I had erased it when I turned the hands of time back three hours.

"He's probably wondering how they caught him," I said. "He thought he was so clever."

"I still can't believe it," Rita whispered through shocked tears. "I thought Sky was my *friend*!"

"I'm shocked too, especially about Kyle! I thought it was *your* boyfriend who was a killer, but it was *mine*! Kyle pretended to care for me, but he only cared about keeping the Mettley secret. When I look back, I realize it must have been Kyle I heard lurking on the beach that night when I walked with Mr. Edwards. He was probably planning to kill Mr. Edwards that night."

"How awful!" Rita said. "Do you think it was Kyle who erased your computer files?"

"It must have been," I said sadly. "He was always trying to get me to forget the past. I guess he was afraid I'd figure things out."

My sister and I hugged and cried and then I said, "If I put it off any longer, I'll change my mind and stay."

So Rita accompanied me to the attic, and before we said good-bye I attempted once more to change fate. "Don't let our father fly in any small planes," I said.

I slipped on my visor and visualized the attic in the year 2070.

28

I RETURNED TO 2070 AND WAS SHOCKED TO LEARN that my short visit to the past had altered the history of the entire planet. My smallest action was like nudging the first domino in a row of dominoes that circled the earth. *Everything* I did—from letting the cat out of the attic to eating a wedge of lemon cake—caused an endless succession of events that influenced the lives of millions of people. Some of the changes were subtle: a house painted blue instead of red, a girl named Dora instead of Doris, a holiday celebrated on the sixteenth of May instead of the seventeenth.

Other changes were more obvious.

Kyle was never born. He was never born because his *father* was never born. Sky Mettley never married, never had sons. He was put to death in 1971 at age 22 for murdering Dr. Crowell.

I did not spill a tear for Kyle. How could I, when I knew what he was capable of? He was every bit the killer his grandfather was. When Kyle had his chance at life, he murdered an innocent old man.

When I prevented Charles Edwards from going blind, I changed the course of his life. Sometimes I sit and gaze at the Charles Edwards painting hanging in our hallway. The sweeping seascape of the calm waters is vividly real—so real it's like looking out the window. The waters are peaceful, but dark threatening clouds creep over the horizon.

They make me think of the dark that nearly closed in on little Chuck Edwards.

"It's an original Charles Edwards!" Mom proudly tells everyone who visits. "He was once a neighbor of my Aunt Ashley's. It's quite valuable, but I'd never dream of selling it. Isn't it a pity he died at eighty when he was caught in that fire at the art gallery? He rushed in to save his paintings and never came out again. I'm sure he had many more wonderful creations in him."

Did I kill Charles Edwards? He died almost thirty years younger because of my interference.

If I think too much about it, it makes me crazy.

Still, I find my thoughts drifting to the missing ones. Where is Ruby? She does not live next door to us. Is she living in some distant state? Did she die young? Or was she never born?

There are so many others who have vanished since I rearranged destiny. Marla Rindler and Josey Bells no longer exist. They've been replaced by two other popular girls with hair like sunshine who stroll down the school hallways, wiggling their bottoms as if they've always ruled the school. No one cares that Josey and Marla are gone.

Of all the missing ones, I felt the worst about Suki. Maybe it's because her life was so miserable and I did nothing to make her happy. Maybe Suki still exists, I thought, in our *other* life. Maybe in another dimension, she and I are part of a world that includes Kyle, Ruby, Marla, and Josey—all of us living the existence we had before I tangled with fate.

If we *are* living a parallel life, I hope I am being nicer to her.

My world is largely populated by people who were not here before I took my time trip. You would think I'd remember them, but I do not. When I returned, it was as if I stepped into someone else's life with no recollection of that person's past. My memories are those of my *other* life. I remember songs that were never written, places I've never been, and people who were never born.

"Honey, did you bump your head or something?" Mom asked worriedly when I asked her who she was talking about when she mentioned her sister Patsy.

Last time around, I did not have an Aunt Patsy.

The father I remember is no longer here. Mom is married to Roy—the man she'd *divorced* in her other life. He is a sandy-haired man with an easy smile who loves to tease me. It's funny, but even though I don't remember him, he seems more like a father than Mom's other husband.

I'm glad he's in our life, and it makes me feel a little better about the ones who are not here. Still, I felt awful about Suki until that afternoon I browsed through the computer files of the Mills family album. There—in a photograph of one of my brother Jim's students—was Suki. It was 1987 and her name was Nan Calacort, but she was definitely Suki. She had the same pale blue eyes and hay-colored hair, but her smile was different. Oh, they were the same lips, but they curved into a confident smile.

It looked as if my visit to Madame Calacort had made an impact. Apparently, she'd reclaimed the embryo and had it implanted in her own womb.

My time trip had another positive effect. Rita succeeded in talking our father into staying out of small planes. He and our mother lived well into their nineties. He got our mother to the doctor in time to catch the deadly cancer.

Though I often reflect on all that's happened, I try to focus on the life I live now. I destroyed the visor, vowing to never take another time trip. Still, I'm forever aware my smallest decision may have a tremendous effect on the future.

Some may argue our future is set for us—laid out like a stone path by an unseen force. But I know differently.

Each time I go to a restaurant and order a glass of juice, I think of Dr. Grady's example. If it is the last glass, will the next customer walk out of the restaurant before he can meet his future wife? Will their child never be born? Would this child have been a great leader or a vicious criminal?

Or perhaps it's not the last glass of juice. But by ordering it, I will cause the waitress to become distracted and forget to serve the side dish of hash brown potatoes to a difficult customer. Will her boss fire her when the customer complains? Will she take another job, only to be in a terrible crash on her way to work?

Or maybe by ordering the juice, I will remind the waitress she needs to stop on the way home and buy juice for her baby. At the store, maybe she'll smile at the old woman shopping for cat food. And her smile will remind the old woman of her granddaughter. The old woman will call that granddaughter, inviting her for a visit. The granddaughter will meet her future husband during the visit, and their child will one day give birth to a doctor who discovers a cure for a disease that enables a great comedian to live, who in turn makes millions of people laugh.

"Think of the chain reactions we cause," I said to my sister. "Everything we do has the potential to change the fate of everyone in the world around us."

"Yes, it is mind-boggling when you stop and think of it," Rita said. Her once chestnut hair now hangs to her waist in smokey curls.

I visit her regularly in her apartment on Deep Brine Island. She's lived there with our brother Jim since Ben died at age 105. After licking his alcohol problem, Ben became a counselor, helping others with addictions. My sister and he raised two daughters, and spoiled five grandchildren, twelve great-grandchildren, twenty-eight great-great-grandchildren, and seven great-great-great-grandchildren.

I hoped Rita would tell me Shane never got over me. But he married right out of high school and eventually became a computer salesman. He and his wife perished together when they fell through an ice pond at age sixty.

I'm glad Shane had someone to love. Yet I feel jealous. In my memory, it has been only weeks since he held me in his arms. He may have married, but I like to think he never forgot me.

Tangling with fate proved to be a painful experience, and I find myself proceeding cautiously. As I told Rita, "Sometimes I worry that everything I say or do will set off a chain reaction that will end with sad consequences."

"Don't let it worry you, dear," she said. "In my long years I've learned that if we go forward with love in our hearts and best intentions for our fellow people, things will usually work out. And if they don't—*que serà serà*. What will be, will be. We can carry in our hearts the knowledge that whatever happens, we meant well."

It is strange to have an older sister who has grown so wise.